As Odell stood listening, another sound reached his ears, and his heart almost stopped beating. Footsteps were coming down the stairway behind him. He was trapped between the men in the room, and the newcomers. He cursed himself for not having brought his service revolver, but that was in the drawer of his desk back in London. He had not visualised a use for it on a peaceful holiday such as he had intended. He braced himself as the footfalls came steadily closer and closer.

The Casebook Of Raymond Odell

Guy N. Smith

Other books by Guy N. Smith:

WEREWOLF OMNIBUS
THE CHARNEL CAVES: A CRABS NOVEL
SABAT 6: THE RETURN
TALES FROM THE GRAVEYARD

Further books by the Sinister Horror Company:

WHAT GOOD GIRLS DO – *Jonathan Butcher*

MARKED – *Stuart Park*

FOREST UNDERGROUND – *Lydian Faust*

CANNIBAL NUNS FROM OUTER SPACE! – *Duncan P. Bradshaw*

PUNCH – *J. R. Park*
DEATH DREAMS IN A WHOREHOUSE – *J. R. Park*
MAD DOG – *J. R. Park*

BREAKING POINT – *Kit Power*

HELL SHIP – *Benedict J. Jones*

MANIAC GODS – *Rich Hawkins*

Visit SinisterHorrorCompany.com for further information on these and other coming titles.

PRESENTS

The Casebook of Raymond Odell

Guy N. Smith

The Casebook of Raymond Odell

Copyright © 2020 by Guy N. Smith

All rights reserved. No part of this publication may be reproduced, distributed or transmitted in any form or by any means, without prior written permission.

Edited by J. R. Park
Design by J. R. Park
Cover art by Mike McGee
Illustrations in *The Case of the Flying Corpse* by Peter Knifton

Published by The Sinister Horror Company

Publisher's Note: This is a work of fiction. Names, characters, places, and incidents are a product of the author's imagination. Locales and public names are sometimes used for atmospheric purposes. Any resemblance to actual people, living or dead, or to businesses, companies, events, institutions, or locales is completely coincidental.

The Casebook of Raymond Odell -- 1st ed.
ISBN 978-1-912578-27-6

ACKNOWLEDGEMENTS

A special thank you to Shane Agnew, Chris Hall and Hal Astell for their research and uncovering the stories of Raymond Odell, including plumbing the depths of their own personal collections to share some unpublished gems.

Also, a big thank you to Pete Knifton for the permission to print the comic strip he drew all those years ago.

THE SINISTER CHAMPIONS

Anthony Watson, Chris Hall,
David Lars Chamberlain, Gary Hooper,
Gothic Alice, James Steel, Jason Kelly,
Jorge Wiles, Matt Shaw, Steve Matthewman
& Thomas Joyce.

Thank you for your support.

To become a Sinister Champion, visit our Patreon page for details at:

www.patreon.com/SinisterHorrorCompany

For Hal Astell who was an invaluable help in the early years of Black Hill Books and the launch of Raymond Odell.
My sincere thanks for all his efforts.

Contents

Introduction	Pg 01
Introducing Raymond Odell	Pg 05
The Making of a Detective	Pg 07
The Fatal Smoke	Pg 25
The Garrotter	Pg 37
Faithful Betrayal	Pg 49
The Curse of the Crystal	Pg 63
Death on the Stairs	Pg 75
Dressed to Kill	Pg 85
Concrete Evidence	Pg 95
Quick-Change Artist	Pg 107

The Case of the Ostrich Slasher	Pg 119
The Bomb	Pg 135
The Perfect Murder	Pg 151
The Poisoners	Pg 165
The Case of the Flying Corpse	Pg 177

Introduction

The later part of the nineteenth century spawned a number of detectives all of whom worked with an assistant. Most famous of all was Conan Doyle's Sherlock Holmes with the faithful Doctor Watson who related each and every case.

Alongside this famous pair Scottish, publishers D.C. Thomson, introduced Dixon Hawke and his young assistant Tommy Burke who lasted through to the present day, and featured in the Saturday edition of their local newspaper. A rival series, Sexton Blake and Tinker, was published as a monthly novelette which ran for around 500 issues.

This then moved on to a series of novels, but times were changing. Around 1990 publishers were discontinuing category fiction in favour of biographies and books on gardening etc. This was when I decided to introduce my own detectives, namely Raymond Odell and his young assistant Tommy Burke.

Whilst I was still penning the occasional Hawke story for D.C. Thomson there was no commercial market for newcomers to a scene which had faded. So I published them in my newsletter Fan Club "Graveyard Rendezvous" and other amateur publications which focused on nostalgia. One has recently featured in my anthology "Tales from the Graveyard".

So, why did I write a number of detective mysteries which were no longer fashionable? I guess it was because I was clinging to nostalgia and wanted to be part of the scene which had fascinated me in my youth. Having been published in numerous genres over the years I wanted to include a pair of detectives to add to these. It is worth mentioning that all these out-dated detective yarns were published gratis in fanzines and amateur booklets. I was never paid for them. I would mention that much thought and time was devoted to them and they gave me a lot of satisfaction.

When it was suggested to me that I might compile a "Case Book" of these long-forgotten mystery yarns I leapt at the idea.

All this has jogged my memory back to my childhood days. Encouraged to write by my mother (E.M. Weale, an historical novelist) I used to compile a handwritten, illustrated, comic book for her on a monthly basis. She used to pay me 10/- (50p) for each issue as a means of encouragement! I have those issues in my private collection and I note that I had created a detective from that era which inspired me even in those early boyhood days. His name was Stan Webster. Maybe one day I will resurrect him…

It has given me great pleasure reviving a forgotten era in this volume.

Enjoy a nostalgic read.

- Guy N. Smith

Guy N. Smith

Introducing Raymond Odell

When one thinks of a private detective one either conjures up a picture of an armchair investigator, shrouded in pipe smoke, peering through a large magnifying lens, or else that of a bronzed handsome man who lives in a world of fast cars and even faster women. Raymond Odell is a mixture of both. He is a 'thinker' as well as a man of action. One day he may solve a problem after hours of meditation, the result being attained through sheer mental perseverance, and the following day may find him on the trail of a dangerous killer with his own life in constant jeopardy.

Odell is both kind and ruthless, his mood determined by the case upon which he is working. His shrewd brain is quick to spot a clue, and accompanied by the faithful Tommy Bourne, whose services he first acquired in 'The Making of a Detective,' and working in conjunction with the gruff, but kindly Detective Inspector Peter Richmond of the C.I.D. in an atmosphere of friendly rivalry, he declares war on the leeches of society. Murderers, blackmailers, forgers and confidence tricksters sleep uneasily at night when Odell is called in on the case. Not only is he a first-class detective, but above all, he understands life.

The Making Of A Detective

The sign above the shop doorway read - 'Rogan & Ryan - Wet Fish Merchants'. The lettering was superfluous, however, for anybody with even the faintest sense of smell

Guy N. Smith

The Making of a Detective

The sign above the shop doorway read - 'Rogan & Ryan - Wet Fish Merchants'. The lettering was superfluous, however, for anybody with even the faintest sense of smell would have detected the presence of the shop the moment that they had set foot in the dingy side street. In a small seaside fishing town, such as Marport, one would have sensed there was something amiss, had there not been a permanent odour of herring and mackerel permeating the place, but the stench from these particular premises was nauseating, to say the least.

The tall man in the polo-necked sweater and corduroy trousers wrinkled his nose as he surveyed the shop in question from the opposite side of the street. It would have been difficult to estimate his age, indeed he could have been anywhere between thirty five and forty five, except that the odd grey hair which was noticeable in the region of his temples would have tempted the outside observer to split the difference and say forty. His wide forehead and aquiline features might have given him a sinister appearance, had his grey eyes not denoted a friendliness, and a keen interest in all that went on about him.

He seemed to come to a decision, and having done so, crossed over the road, and made towards the doorway whence came the obnoxious odours. A bell jangled sharply from somewhere at the rear of the premises as he pushed open the door and stepped into the semi-darkness of the evil smelling fish-shop. Seconds later the young assistant, the one who had delivered the weekly order at his lodgings earlier on in the day, appeared on the scene. Tommy Bourne, for that was his name, was pulling on a grubby pair of overalls, and his old school cap was perched on the back of his head. The friendly smile on his freckled face showed a genuine welcome.

'Hallo, again sir,' he greeted, 'Didn't think I'd see you again, so soon. I know it's an awful cheek, sir and I might be quite wrong, but I was going to ask you if by any chance you were.....'

Before he could finish the sentence, a burly red-haired man appeared behind him, roughly pushing him to one side. 'Go and finish loading the van, Bourne,' he bullied. 'I told you I'd watch the shop. That delivery's got to be made before five o'clock.' The youth turned away to do his bidding, and the man turned to his customer. 'And what can I do for you, chum?' he attempted to sound friendly now, and what was intended to be a smile showed a row of broken and blackened teeth.

'I would like to know,' the customer was quite unperturbed, 'how long lobsters have been wearing nylon stockings.'

For some moments there was a pregnant silence, and during this time the tall man pulled a small polythene bag from his pocket, undid the rubber bands which secured it into a small bundle, and unrolled a pair of good quality ladies nylon stockings from it. He laid them out on the counter in front of him and stood surveying them in silence. 'These,' he continued, 'were inside one of the lobsters which you delivered to my landlady at No. 10 Harcombe Court, this morning. In another, one of the guests found an opal, which he is holding in safe keeping pending the owner claiming it.'

'I'll fetch you another box of lobsters,' the shopkeeper's ruddy complexion had suddenly gone several shades paler. 'I don't know what has gone wrong, but I'll endeavour to find out.'

As he turned away, Bourne re-appeared in the doorway, a box of kippers in his arms.

'Oh, lor!' he gasped evidently having heard part of the conversation. 'I've dropped a clanger again have I? Must have got the orders mixed up Mr. Rogan.'

'You stupid oaf,' the man who was obviously one of the partners in the business gave a roar of rage, and lashed the youth across the side of the head with his ham like fist. 'You can have your cards on Saturday. This is the third time this week you've got the orders mixed up. All you can think about is reading those penny dreadfuls — Sexton Blake, Dixon Hawke, bah! What a load of rubbish you waste your time on! Well after this week you'll have plenty of time for reading.'

'I believe the lobsters were intended for Doctor Caston,' the customer seemed quite unperturbed, except for the fact that his eyes were keenly scrutinising the other's face.

'How d'you know that?' Hogan was almost beside himself with rage.

'His name was on the box they came in,' was the reply, 'so I presume that was who they were intended for.'

'It's none of your damned business who they were meant for,' bellowed Regan, pushing a small wooden box of lobsters across the counter. 'You've got nothing to complain about anyway. Here, take these and clear off. You've got double what you ordered for the same price.'

The tall man calmly picked up the box, tucked it under his arm, and without a further word he turned on his heel and left the shop. The moment the door had closed behind him, Regan turned on the young assistant in a terrible fury.

'You young fool,' he stormed, 'I even write the customers names on the orders as well as the addresses, and even then you can't get your deliveries right!'

The youth was tenderly rubbing the side of his face where the blow had caught him. He looked at his employer, and a grin began to form on his face. 'I bet you don't know who that was,' he retorted, 'if you spent some of your time reading you might have recognised him.'

'I don't give a damn who he was,' the fish-merchant began to lose his temper once again, and then suddenly a puzzled look crossed his face. His voice became quieter, as he asked. 'Who was he, anyway?'

'Well,' Tommy Bourne, began to regain some of his lost confidence, 'I wouldn't swear to it of course, but I've seen his picture in the papers enough times, and I'd say that was Raymond Odell, the private detective from London. You know a sort of real-life Sherlock Holmes, helps the police from time to time. I read once...'

But Rogan was no longer listening. His face was even whiter than when the stranger had first placed the nylons on the counter, and his hand was shaking uncontrollably as he staggered into the back room, picked up the receiver of the telephone and began dialling a number.

There was no moon that night, and Raymond Odell was grateful for that fact, as he silently made his way through the large shrubberies which bordered Earlsdon Manor, the large rambling house which was situated on the cliff tops above Marport. He moved with the stealth of one who was accustomed to being abroad at night. His wartime training with the Commandos had served him well, and he gently tested the ground with his foot at each step, before putting his full weight on it. He had no desire to betray his presence by carelessly cracking a dead twig or disturbing a cluster of stones. Perhaps he should have telephoned Scotland Yard, and told Detective Inspector Richmond of his discoveries and suspicions whilst holidaying in this quiet little seaside resort, but that was not Odell's way. He had always been a lone wolf. Richmond could come in at the kill, when he had verified his suspicions.

The catch on the small window at the rear of the building offered no obstacle to the detective, and within a matter of minutes he had forced an entry, and lowered himself into, what he judged, was the larder. He dared risk only a brief flesh of his pencil torch, merely to get his bearings, and then he was in darkness again.

The larder door was unlocked, and he silently passed through it into a narrow corridor. Using the wall as a guide he decided to head to the right, his sense of direction telling him that this would lead him into the heart of the building.

He passed two heavy oak doors, but as he gently tried the handles of each, he found that they were locked. It would have taken too long to discover the mechanism of the locks, and pick them, particularly as the rooms in question might not warrant the work involved. At the end of the corridor he came to a flight of stone steps, leading downwards. Some sort of a cellar, I suppose, he thought to himself, and then for the first time he heard voices. They were men's voices, coming from below, and were muffled to such an extent that he was unable to distinguish any words.

Step by step he descended the narrow steps. It was almost as if they were a spiral staircase hewn out of the very cliffs below the house, and the rougher they became, the more certain Odell was that this was indeed the case.

Suddenly, on rounding a bend, he came face to face with a thick wooden door and noticed a shaft of light filtering out from under it. The voices were louder now, and he could plainly hear what they were saying as he stood there, scarcely daring to breath.

There was a meeting of some sort taking place in the room behind the door, and it seemed to be dominated by a man with a highly cultured voice, interspersed by grunts of approval from the listeners.

'This man Odell will put us on the spot.' Raymond Odell started as the words reached him. 'At midnight there will be the usual delivery from the yacht. Dispose of it as usual. An hour before dawn a launch will arrive with a special delivery including several operatives from the other side, and at dawn you will all travel by truck under Ryan's orders. Obey them to the very letter. This is our final job. We dare not risk it any longer.'

As Odell stood listening another sound reached his ears, and his heart almost stopped beating. Footsteps were coming down the stairway behind him. He was trapped between the men in the room, and the newcomers. He cursed himself for not having brought his service revolver, but that was in the drawer of his desk back in London. He had not visualised a use for it on a peaceful holiday such as he had intended. He braced himself as the footfalls came steadily closer and closer.

He came to an instant decision. He had to clash with one of the parties, and out of choice it had better be the one with the least number of people in it. He knew that there were at least four or five men behind the door, but, as far as he could tell from the footsteps, there were no more than two newcomers. It would therefore, have to be the latter which he clashed with.

After what seemed an eternity, the footsteps were almost upon him. He held his breath, timing his moment of action to take place just as the two men rounded the bend. His left fist shot out like a steam-driven piston, and he felt it sink home in somebody's stomach. He wasted no time in self satisfaction, however, and using his element of surprise to the full, brought his right hand into action, using a downward chopping movement which caught the second man across the neck. Two down, and time to go!

The disturbance had already been heard by the men in the room, and Odell was not waiting to take on any more of the gang. He took the steps two at a time in his wild dash for freedom, and seconds later he was back in the corridor above. He paused for a second in order to obtain his bearings, and then there was a blinding flash from somewhere inside his head. The blackness which enveloped him was more than the darkness in which he stood. It was sheer oblivion, and he pitched forward without a sound.

Odell regained consciousness by having a bucket of water thrown over him. Even in his semi-conscious state he could taste the salt, and knew for a fact that it was sea water that he had been doused with. With an effort he opened his eyes. His head throbbed, and it was some seconds before his brain was capable of understanding the scene before him.

His hands were bound tightly behind him, and he sprawled on the beach in the cove below Earlsdon Manor. Dawn was just breaking, and in the dim light he saw a group of six or seven rough looking men clad in sweaters, standing over him. A motor launch was moored some distance from the shore, and one of the men were holding a rubber dinghy.

'So you've come round, have you, Mr. Clever Odell?' Odell recognised the cultured voice, which he had heard inside the house, and forced his eyes to focus on the speaker. He was a tall, good looking man, dressed in a light grey suit, and smoking a large cigar.

'Good evening, Doctor Caston,' the detective said, attempting to keep his voice even, for he had no doubt in his mind that this was the owner of Earlsdon Manor, and the ringleader of the smuggling ring.

'You seem to have shown a great interest in our activities,' the doctor went on, 'and as a reward for your labours my foreign friends are going to take you aboard their launch. They are leaving for the continent in a few moments, and you will be accompanying them... but not all the way!'

The implication behind his words was only too plain. As soon as they were clear of the coast they would drop the bound detective overboard, and that would be that, reflected Odell.

Two rough looking men dressed in shabby seafaring clothes hauled him to his feet, and began pushing him towards the water's edge, where another of the gang had the inflatable rubber dinghy afloat.

'Put him in and get him out to the launch,' barked Caston.

Whee- ping! Something that seemed like an angry hornet whizzed between the group of men, and with a hissing noise the rubber craft began to deflate.

'What the..!' began Caston, but before he could finish a second missile followed in the wake of the first, burying itself with a distinctive 'plop' in his fleshy cheek. He screamed in agony, clasping his hand to his face, all else forgotten.

Ping-Ping-whee-ee-plop! The silent missiles seemed to be coming from all directions and Raymond Odell flung himself on to the sand, and lying flat, prayed that he would not be hit. Men were scattering everywhere, seeking any available cover in an effort to get away from these flying messengers of destruction.

The detective rolled over on his side, and looked towards the cliffs, and as he did so, his heart gave a leap, and for one moment he thought that he must be dreaming. Never had he seen such a welcome sight. Carefully picking their way down the narrow path which led from the cliff above, were a dozen or so uniformed policemen, three Alsatians, and a tall well-built man in civvies who led the way, and seemed to be in charge of operations.

'Cops!' the yell went up from one of the smugglers crouching amidst the scattered rocks of the small cove. However, there was nothing that they could do about it. The rubber dinghy was useless and their only other escape route was blocked by the men in blue.

Raymond Odell watched as the police, aided by the dogs, carried out a systematic round up. The plain clothes man, his trilby hat perched on the back of his head, spotted the bound detective and came across to cut him free.

'You must be Odell,' he said, as his pocketknife slashed through the cords. 'We had a telephone message telling us that you were in trouble at Earlsdon Manor, but when we arrived the place was empty. One of my men spotted a group of people on the beach, and then all hell seemed to be let loose. We just came in as a clearing up operation.'

'Who 'phoned you?' asked Odell, and then his eyes travelled past the policeman to where a youth of about sixteen years of age had just emerged from behind a pile of rocks, close to the rocky path leading from the cliffs above. In his hand he carried a black shiny .177 air pistol, the latest type which was being sold in sports shops all over the country, and its makers claimed that it was capable of firing fifteen shots without reloading. A broad grin was on his freckled face as he walked towards the two men.

'Tommy Bourne!' gasped Odell.

Two hours later, after a hearty breakfast in the police canteen, Raymond Odell and Tommy Bourne sat in the office of Inspector Watson, the man who had led the rescue party at Earlsdon Cove.

'I guessed there was something fishy going on,' Tommy replied, in answer to the Inspector's question. 'When I recognised Mr. Odell in the shop, and Mr. Rogan was so furious because I'd delivered Doctor Caston's lobsters to the wrong address, I thought I would take a look round there tonight.'

'Sexton Blake would have done that wouldn't he?' smiled Raymond Odell, his keen eyes noticing the cheap novelette hastily crammed in the pocket of the youth's jacket.

'I saw you go into the Manor through the window,' Tommy went on, and when you didn't show up in about an hour I nipped back to the nearest 'phone box, 'phoned the police, and then went back up to the Manor, as I got back they were dragging you down to the cove. I followed, and when I saw what they were going to do, I thought I'd better start shooting at the rubber dinghy for a start.' He grinned, 'Aunt Rose, I live with her 'cause I've got no parents, bought me the pistol for my birthday last week.'

'And a very good job she did, too,' smiled Raymond Odell, 'I really walked into the lion's den last night. If it hadn't been for you my number might have been up, Tommy.'

The inspector smiled too, he would get the credit for the capture of the gang, and that was all that mattered to him.

'You've no job now have you Tommy?' Raymond Odell said after a moment or two of silence, 'I mean with Rogan and Ryan going to prison along with Doctor Caston, the shop will be closed.'

'I guess so,' a look of despondency came over the youth's face.

'How would you fancy working as a private detective's assistant?' Odell asked.

'Gosh!' Tommy Bourne half rose from his seat in excitement. 'D'you really mean it, Mr. Odell?'

'I do.' Odell stated, leaving no room for doubt in the other's mind. 'I could use a young man like you back in London. I think you've got the makings of a detective, given the right training. Mind you, it's mostly routine work with plenty of menial tasks, but we do get the odd bit of excitement from time to time. I thought perhaps that, as you've no ties here in Marport now, you might like to come back to London with me at the end of the week. I'm strictly on holiday at the moment.'

'I'll go and tell Aunt Rose at once, and get a few things together, Mr. Odell.' Tommy was already on his way to the door. As he passed the large metal wastepaper basket something thudded into it.

Sexton Blake was finished. Fiction had been replaced by fact.

The Fatal Smoke

Raymond Odell, the famous Dover Street detective, and his young assistant, Tommy Bourne, had been to the theatre for the evening. It had been a good show.

Guy N. Smith

The Fatal Smoke

Raymond Odell, the famous Dover Street detective, and his young assistant, Tommy Bourne, had been to the theatre for the evening. It had been a good show, but most of all the two had enjoyed the relaxation of the few hours away from the problems which beset them daily. They left the tube, and piled into the large elevator, along with twenty or so other people. There seemed a general air of gaiety and laughter, such as one will find during the late hours in London, when everybody seems bent only on enjoying themselves.

The lift came to a halt, and as the gates opened, people surged forward. Odell and Tommy stood back to avoid the rush, and as they did so they noticed a man standing in the far corner of the elevator. He was finding it difficult to remain upright, and his eyes were closed as he attempted to grasp at the smooth walls behind him. Then, with a final moan, he sank to the floor, a lighted cigarette falling from his fingers as he did so.

Raymond Odell was kneeling by his side almost immediately. The man's trilby hat had fallen off, revealing a mass of dark grey hair, and the Dover Street detective put his age at about fifty.

'He's dead!' Odell snapped. 'Go and 'phone for a doctor and the police, Tommy, whilst I stop here with him.'

As Tommy Bourne dashed off to do his chief's bidding, Odell noticed that he was completely alone. Their fellow passengers had been so eager to leave the lift that they had not noticed the man's condition, and by leaving the lift gates open, Odell ensured that it could not be recalled for further use. Systematically he began an examination of the dead man's pockets in an attempt to identify him. Suddenly, he bent down, and sniffed at the man's mouth. A puzzled look crossed his face, and then he noticed the stub of the cigarette smouldering on the floor close by. He picked it up, and when the same bitter odour reached his nostrils, a steely glint came into his eyes.

'Cyanide poisoning,' he murmured. 'A doped cigarette!'

A search of the dead man's pockets revealed that he was Harry Richardson, a company director, residing in Hendon. He also found a packet of ten 'Champion' cigarettes, containing only nine of the neat white cylinders. He sniffed at them, but could detect no trace of poison in any of them. 'So only one contained poison,' he muttered to himself. 'Very interesting.'

Ten minutes later Tommy Bourne returned, accompanied by two uniformed police officers, and a police doctor who was well acquainted with Raymond Odell. A few seconds later their old friend and ally, Detective-Inspector Richmond of Scotland Yard, arrived, and quickly the Dover Street detective explained his findings.

'I'm inclined to agree with Mr. Odell,' the police doctor stated after a cursory examination. 'Naturally, I can't be sure without a post mortem, but it seems a clear case of cyanide poisoning to me.'

'We'd better take a trip out to Hendon,' Richmond stated. 'Perhaps you'd like to accompany us, Odell. If this chap Richardson's got a wife she'll have to be told, and anyway we've got to try and find out whose company he's been in this evening, if anybody's.'

Half an hour later the police car pulled up outside a row of very modest, detached houses in Hendon, and Richmond rang the bell. A small neat woman, whom they judged to be in her late fifties, answered the ring. She was clad in a dressing-gown, and was obviously on the point of retiring for the night. As gently as possible, Richmond broke the news to her. She took it bravely, and after a few minutes steeled herself to answer the inevitable questions.

'My husband had a greengrocery business,' she stated in reply to Richmond's questions. 'He was in partnership with a man named Brighthouse. They had an office in the city, and had been out tonight drinking with a couple of other fellows. I can't tell you the names of these other gentlemen, I'm afraid. They had so many business acquaintances in the city, but Mr. Brighthouse lives in Norwood, and I can give you his address.'

Walter Brighthouse was a flabby individual, a few years younger than Richardson, and he was already in bed when the detectives called upon him. He came downstairs eventually and ushered them into the living room. He produced a silver cigarette case from the pocket of his dressing gown, selected and lit one, and inhaled deeply.

'Dead!' he gasped when he heard the news. 'I can't believe it. He was alright when I got off the tube and left him. I can give you the addresses of Joe Ellison and Jim Carter, whom we spent the evening with in 'Sid's Bar', if it's any help to you.'

Jim Carter, who gave Raymond Odell the impression of a city spiv, also had to be called from his bed. He, too, received the news with a certain amount of surprise, and the Dover Street detectives noticed that he smoked 'Golden Eagle' cigarettes, as he nervously pulled one out of a packet, and lit it.

'I think we had better conduct this interview at Scotland Yard,' Richmond said. 'It will be simpler for all concerned, and we can pick up Joe Ellison on the way in.'

Two hours later the two Dover Street detectives were seated in Detective-Inspector Richmond's room at Scotland Yard, where they listened to their official colleague questioning Carter and Ellison. Raymond Odell leaned across and spoke to Richmond in a low voice. 'I think we ought to complete the party and have Brighthouse here,' he said. 'Also the bar-owner, Sid!'

'As you wish,' Richmond replied. 'I don't really see the necessity for it, but I'll ring through and have a car go and pick them up if you like.'

Odell listened intently whilst Jim Carter told how they had met in Sid's Bar about 10.00 p.m. Carter was an accountant and had worked at his office until nearly that time. He audited the accounts for Richardson and Brighthouse, and the meeting was purely a business one, until Joe Ellison turned up shortly before closing time.

Joe Ellison merely confirmed what they already knew. They had all travelled home on the same line. He and Carter got off before Richardson and Brighthouse.

There was an interruption as a uniformed constable ushered in an irate Brighthouse, and a sharp faced little man who was none other than the proprietor of Sid's Bar.

Brighthouse was annoyed at being sent for a second time for questioning, but Odell ignored him as he began interviewing Sid.

'Did you sell any cigarettes to any of the four gentlemen?' the Dover Street detective asked.

'Indeed, I did,' the other replied. 'Mr. Richardson never fails to buy a packet of ten 'Champions' whenever he drinks in my place. I stock them for him, actually, because there's very little call for them otherwise. I believe the others each bought a packet of 'Golden Eagles."

'I see,' Raymond Odell lit his pipe, and as he puffed out clouds of blue smoke, Tommy and Richmond noticed a glint in his eyes which they knew only too well. He was on to something. 'This is the way I see it,' he went on. 'Four men are gathered in a small bar. Two of them buy a packet of cigarettes each, both different brands. Now, one of the three knew that Richardson only smoked 'Champion' cigarettes, so he took along with him a packet of ten, containing one dosed with cyanide. It would be a fairly easy matter to substitute this packet for the one Richardson had just bought, in the crush at the bar. Four men left the bar at about 10.50 p.m., one of them with a packet of 'Champions' in his pocket, with the dosed cigarette amongst it. Two of the others had a packet of 'Golden Eagle' and the packet of 'Champions' which he had taken from Richardson, in order to substitute for the killer packet. He would have been wiser to have thrown these cigarettes away. Now, gentlemen, I would be glad if you would all place your cigarettes on the desk in front of you!'

Ellison and Carter somewhat hesitantly placed packets of 'Golden Eagle' cigarettes on Richmond's desk. Brighthouse fumbled in his pockets, and then shook his head. 'Sorry gentlemen,' he blustered, 'but in the rush of being dragged from my bed for a second time tonight, I have come without mine.'

Odell smiled grimly. 'Not to worry, Mr. Brighthouse,' he said, 'I know what brand they would have been. They would have been a packet of 'Golden Eagles', and the packet of 'Champion' which you took from Richardson's pocket earlier tonight in Sid's Bar!'

'You're bluffing!' snarled Brighthouse, leaping to his feet. 'You can't prove a thing.'

'Indeed, I can,' retorted Raymond Odell.

'You see, I already saw you smoke a 'Champion' tonight. I noticed it because the makers of these cigarettes print the name *across* the cigarette, close to the end. 'Golden Eagle', however, print their name along the *length* of the cigarette. I was thus able to identify your smoke from a distance, although at that time the significance had not dawned on me. It's a pity for you that 'Champion' are not more popular and smoked generally.'

Two uniformed policemen were already entering the room in answer to the bell which Richmond had pressed.

'Excellent observation on your part, Odell,' praised Detective-Inspector Richmond when he called in at the Dover Street consulting room a couple of days later. 'Brighthouse has confessed to Richardson's murder. Apparently, he had been fiddling the books, and, with an audit imminent, he became desperate. He planned Richardson's death to look like suicide, but it was rather a clumsy effort. We've since found Brighthouse's fingerprints on the packet of cigarettes which contained the fatal one.'

'Well, he'll deserve all he gets,' Raymond Odell replied. 'Richardson may well have offered his cigarettes to a friend or business acquaintance. There was no certainty that he would smoke the one intended for him.'

Guy N. Smith

The Garrotter

'If you can spare us some of your time, Mr. Odell, we shall be more than grateful to you.' The speaker was Chief-Inspector Donnington of the Wilmington-on-Sea police force.

Guy N. Smith

The Garrotter

'If you can spare us some of your time, Mr. Odell, we shall be more than grateful to you.' The speaker was Chief-Inspector Donnington of the Wilmington-on-Sea police force, and he was addressing Raymond Odell, the famous Dover Street detective, and his young assistant, Tommy Bourne, who were holidaying in the area. They were seated round the desk in the interview room of the Wilmington police station, and the only other person present was a balding man in his late fifties. This latter was Stan Rippon, Editor-in-Chief of the Wilmington Herald.

'No doubt you've read about the Wilmington murders in the national dailies, Mr. Odell,' Donnington went on. 'There's a maniacal strangler at large, and he always sends prior notice of his intended killings to the press. At first we thought it was all a hoax. Now he's threatened twice and killed twice. Both his victims have been local shop-girls. I was speaking to Scotland Yard about it this morning, and a fellow there by the name of Detective-Inspector Richmond of the C.I.D. seemed to know you well, and advised me to get in touch with you as you were staying in the area. If you can spare us the time...'

'I'm only too pleased to lend a hand,' Raymond Odell replied. 'Now, what's the latest on this strangler?'

'We've had another letter this morning,' Rippon cut in. 'He always writes to our offices, never to the police. Seems he likes publicity. I'll read it out to you. "I shall be striking again tonight (Saturday) in the Tinkers Green area." There's no signature, as usual.'

'I've already alerted extra police and specials,' Donnington said. 'Perhaps you'd like to accompany me in my car, Mr. Odell, and your assistant, of course.'

'I'm game,' Odell replied. 'If you'd like to pick us up at the Seaview Hotel after dinner, we'll be ready.'

When Chief-Inspector Donnington called for Odell and Tommy just after 8.00 p.m., he had in the car with him Stan Rippon and 'Splash' Wharton, the chief reporter of the Wilmington Herald. The latter was a dumpy little man approaching retiring age and had worked for the paper for years. They cruised down to the Tinkers Green area at the far end of the promenade, and Odell and the inspector remained in the car, in order to receive any messages which might come over the radio, whilst the other three set out, separately, on foot, to mingle with the crowds of late night revellers.

It was a warm late September evening, and Tommy had a job to convince himself that his main job was to keep a sharp watch for anything suspicious which might enable him to recognise the murderer amongst the milling crowds. Naturally the publication of the strangler's letter in the evening editions had helped to draw the people to this place.

It was 11.15 when Tommy reported back to the police car. So far everything was quiet, and Odell and Donnington were enjoying a quiet smoke. Shortly afterwards Rippon and Wharton joined them.

'Looks as if it was a hoax after....' Donnington's words were cut short as the radio crackled into life: '…body found in Lovers' Lane, Tinkers Green.'

The inspector had already pressed the starter, and seconds later their car was hurtling in the direction of Lovers' Lane, its flashing blue light scattering all before it. Ten minutes later they arrived at their destination, a tree-lined lane leading down to the beach. Crowds had already begun to gather, and uniformed policemen and specials were cordoning the area off. The inspector leapt from his car and, followed by Odell, Tommy and the two newspapermen, he forced his way through the crowd.

A constable was shining his torch on the body of a middle-aged special constable lying on the edge of the long grass. 'Bad job sir,' the uniformed man addressed his superior. 'It's Constable Jack White of the specials. This killer must be a tremendously strong man to be able to get the better of him.'

THE GARROTTER

Raymond Odell wheeled round as a strangled cry sounded at his elbow. It was 'Splash' Wharton, and the chief reporter was white and shaking.

'Jack White!' he gasped. 'Oh, no. We were in the Home Guard together as instructors of unarmed combat. My old buddy!'

'Right,' said Raymond Odell, lighting his pipe, and looking across the desk at Chief-Inspector Donnington. 'Let's put a few facts together and see what conclusion we arrive at.'

This time only the Dover Street detectives were present along with Donnington. The two newspapermen had returned to the Herald offices to write up their reports in time for the early editions.

'We know that this strangler uses a method known as garrotting, i.e. the strangulation is carried out without leaving any finger marks on the neck. This is a skilled method of killing, known mostly to the Japs, and also taught to our commandos during the war. Now, the next time a letter from the strangler arrives at the Herald offices, try and persuade Rippon to suppress it. The killer has a dual motive in this besides publicity. The greater the crowds, the easier is his task, for he can move easily amongst crowds of strangers.'

'I'll try and do what you ask,' Donnington replied. 'What's your plan then?'

'We can't exactly make a plan in a case like this,' Odell replied, 'but with fewer people about, our task of watching will be made easier.'

It was almost a week before another letter arrived at the offices of the Wilmington Herald. The strangler was about to strike again. He chose a Saturday night, as before, but this time he would be operating in the Long Sands area of Wilmington, the opposite end of the promenade to Tinkers Green.

'But it's in the interests of the public to print it!' roared an irate Rippon, when he called at the police station, and saw Chief-Inspector Donnington.

'Well, I'm ordering you not to,' snapped the policeman, and glared balefully after the editor as he stalked outside to his car.

However, nine o'clock on the following evening found Odell, Tommy, and both men from the Herald, sitting in Donnington's parked car on the windswept promenade. The weather had changed during the week and had the Dover Street detectives not had a reason for staying on in Wilmington they would have returned to London before now.

THE GARROTTER

'You know, guvnor,' Tommy Bourne said suddenly, as he made to get out of the car and walk the area, as on the previous week, 'I've a shrewd idea who this killer might be.'

'Oh!' replied Raymond Odell. 'Who's that, then, Tommy?'

Four pairs of eyes looked questioningly in the direction of the young detective.

'Well,' replied Tommy. 'I think I'll keep it to myself for the time being. I may be wrong, but let's wait and see what happens tonight, shall we?'

'Where the dickens have all these crowds come from?' Odell asked his official colleague as he saw large numbers of holiday-makers hanging about on the promenade.

'That's queer,' Donnington replied. 'The letter wasn't published in the paper this time. I'd say somebody's been spreading rumours. Probably the strangler himself, for nobody else knew about it, apart from the police and the press.'

Tommy Bourne had now wandered away from the crowds, and the main thoroughfare. The killer had struck in a lonely lane before, and it was a possibility that he would do so again. The young detective paused on the corner of a deserted beach road, undecided which way to go, when he heard a stealthy footfall behind him.

'Got a light, mate?' The voice somehow sounded vaguely familiar, and the dumpy outline of the man in the shadows reminded him of somebody he knew, but before Tommy Bourne could reply, the man had moved with unbelievable speed for his bulk, and two steely hands were encircling the young Dover Street detective's neck. He was like a toy puppet in the hands of his attacker, who could be none other than the garrotter himself.

Tommy's brain began to reel and he felt consciousness slipping away from him, when he suddenly heard the patter of running feet. The stranglehold was suddenly released, and as he fell dazed to the ground, he was aware of a struggle taking place, and then ending as suddenly as it had begun. He shook himself and struggled to his feet.

'Alright, Tommy?' There was no mistaking Raymond Odell's voice.

'Just about, guvnor,' he managed a grin. 'Did you get him?'

'We did,' the Dover Street detective replied, shining his torch on the man who stood handcuffed between Chief-Inspector Donnington and the two uniformed constables. 'That' s him!'

"Splash' Wharton,' gasped Tommy Bourne, unbelievingly.

THE GARROTTER

* * *

'I've had my suspicions of Wharton since last Saturday,' Raymond Odell said, later that night in the Wilmington police station. 'I will never forget the shock he received when he saw that the murdered man at Tinkers Green was special constable Jack White. This is often the case when a maniacal killer suffers from a split-mind. When he returns to his normal mental state, he has fits of remorse. Wharton did this when he saw that he'd killed Jack White. But another clue arose from this particular killing. Jack White was a tremendously strong man, and I wondered how it was that the killer had managed to get the better of him. Then it dawned on me. He must have known the man so well and been engaged in conversation with him so that he never suspected a thing until it was too late. Then again, both Wharton and White were Home-Guard instructors in unarmed combat. Where better to learn the art of garroting? I suspected Wharton then, and when I tipped Tommy off to pass that chance remark about having an idea who the killer was, I figured that he may try to silence him before he had a chance to talk further. That was why, inspector, I was so keen for us to keep my assistant in sight as far as possible tonight. It's certainly a good job that we did.'

'It is indeed,' Chief-Inspector Donnington replied. 'How fortunate, though, for us, that you happened to be staying in Wilmington-on-Sea, Mr. Odell. Well, I suppose you will be glad to continue your holiday now.'

'I shall indeed,' Raymond Odell laughed. 'But I shall be returning to Dover Street for the remainder of it. It's more peaceful there.'

Faithful Betrayal

'It always amazes me,' said Raymond Odell, the famous private detective, 'how seldom schoolmasters are murdered.'
'It always flabbergasts me,' replied Tommy Bourne, his young assistant, 'why a good many more don't get done!'

Guy N. Smith

Faithful Betrayal

'It always amazes me,' said Raymond Odell, the famous private detective, 'how seldom schoolmasters are murdered.'

'It always flabbergasts me,' replied Tommy Bourne, his young assistant, 'why a good many more don't get done!'

Raymond Odell was at the wheel of their powerful car, speeding towards the south coast, in answer to an urgent summons from Detective-

Inspector Richmond of Scotland Yard. Richmond was conducting inquiries into the murder of the headmaster of a small private school. Apparently the Yard man was not having the rapid results he had hoped for in what, at first, seemed to be a straightforward inquiry. In view of some recent successes which the Dover Street detective had obtained for him, Richmond had had no hesitation in calling in his friend once more.

'This must be the place,' murmured Odell, as they came upon some red brick buildings, surrounded by a high wall. The blue sea sparkled in the background. 'Strangehurst School - what a peaceful setting for a ghastly murder.'

As Odell brought the car to a halt in the quadrangle, Richmond emerged from a building close by and came across to meet them.

'Glad you could get here,' he said, shaking the detective by the hand. 'Not such a simple job as I thought it would be when the local inspector sent for me. The body's been taken away by now, of course. It happened on Thursday night. The doctor puts the time of death down at somewhere between eleven and midnight. Walters, the headmaster, was working late in his study. He's a bachelor, so naturally he wasn't missed until the following morning. The killer entered by the unlocked French windows, crept up on the unsuspecting victim, and killed him with a blow from one of a pair of Indian clubs which were on the table in the room. He forced a drawer of the desk and got away with almost one hundred pounds in one pound notes, which were the staff wages due to be paid the following day. I'd like you to have a look at the scene of the crime, and then have a word with the two principal men in the case - Patrick Norton, the second master, who is acting headmaster at the moment, and Ted Woods, the janitor, who is working out his notice. He was given a week's notice, two days ago, by Walters.'

The study was typical of any headmasters' in most private schools. The shelves were lined with books covering a majority of different subjects. The old-fashioned desk was littered with correspondence, and some cricket and hockey gear lay untidily in a heap in one corner.

Raymond Odell began a thorough investigation of the room, using his powerful lens frequently. Tommy and Richmond watched him intently, and they could tell from his expression that he was not having much success. Suddenly he stooped down and paid close attention to the linoleum covered floor. Studying the surface through his magnifying glass he crawled on his hands and knees back to the French windows.

'Did you notice one or two faint footmarks, Richmond?' he asked, keeping his attention focused on the floor.

'They've been photographed,' the Yard man replied. 'They were made, in all probability, by a man wearing running pumps. There are about two hundred pairs in daily use around the school!'

'And these chippings of slate?' the Dover Street detective asked, taking an envelope from his pocket, and carefully dropping two very small pieces of slate chippings into it. He could tell by Richmond's silence that they had either not been noticed, or else disregarded altogether.

Odell was now on his feet, examining the curtains on the open French window. Suddenly they saw him pluck something from one of them and hold it up to the light. It was a single strand of hair, blue-grey in colour. Richmond stepped forward, an eager light in his eyes.

'You must have eyes like an eagle,' he muttered. 'How far from the ground was it?'

'About five feet,' was the reply.

'Then it looks as if we want a short man with grey hair,' Richmond grunted.

'Don't let's jump to hasty conclusions,' Odell warned him. 'Now, if you'll direct me, I'll take Tommy with me, and go and interview those two men. I think perhaps it might be better if we went on our own. It's more informal, and they may talk more freely to us than to the official force.'

Patrick Norton, the second master, was also a bachelor, and lived in a small detached staff bungalow at the furthest boundary of the school grounds. As Odell and Tommy walked up the narrow path of slate chippings to the front door, the schoolmaster opened the door to greet them. He was neatly, but plainly dressed, in a brown sports jacket, and flannels. He was all of six feet tall, completely bald, and cleanshaven.

'It's very disturbing for everyone in the school,' Norton said, when they were all seated in his small lounge. 'I'd like to draw your attention to something I did not mention to the police, Mr. Odell. One is always reluctant to incriminate one's own colleagues, but I suppose you know Ted Woods, the janitor, is working out his notice. He has been pilfering. It has always been his job to go to the bank, and cash the wages cheque on a Thursday. Due to the present unpleasant circumstances I went this week. Then, on Thursday night, as I sometimes do, I rang down to the Lodge to make sure that the main gates were closed for the night. I sometimes check up on him. His wife answered the 'phone. He wasn't there, Mr. Odell! It's troubled me. It seems a terrible thing to have to tell the police. It's almost like turning the key in his cell door!'

It was a bad-tempered Ted Woods who opened the front door of the Lodge to the Dover Street detective. He was a short, thick-set man, with grey hair, and a small moustache. With reluctance he asked them inside. The room was small, and only furnished with bare necessities. His wife was out shopping, he informed Odell.

'Where were you between eleven o'clock and midnight on Thursday night?' the detective casually asked the janitor during the course of ordinary conversation.

'You mind yer own business!' Woods snarled, his face red with anger. 'I didn't do the old goat in, and I got nothin' to account for, and nothin' to be afraid of. And I'll be blowed if I'm goin' to account for my movements to a lot of prying busybodies!'

Tommy Bourne was surprised when his chief merely shrugged his shoulders and stood up to go. It was unlike Odell to abandon his enquiries with such casualness.

On the way to the door, Odell struck a match to light his pipe. In doing so, the matchbox slipped from his fingers. As he stooped down to retrieve it he also picked up a small brightly coloured feather which was lying on the stone quarries. Seconds later the Dover Street sleuths were outside and walking back to the main school buildings.

'Any luck?' queried Richmond, as Odell and Tommy entered the room that the Yard man was using for his temporary headquarters.

'I don't know,' mused Odell, and the official man knew better than to press him further. Raymond Odell would reveal his findings when it suited him, and not until.

'I'm just going out for a short walk first, round the school grounds,' Odell continued. 'Tommy can come with me. With any luck we should be back in an hour or so.'

Tommy Bourne had no idea what they were looking for as they appeared to stroll aimlessly round the grounds. Boys passed them on their way to and from various classes. Tommy received many envious looks, for almost every boy there would have changed places with him, given the chance. Raymond Odell was a household name, even at Strangehurst School.

Suddenly the Dover Street detective stopped in his tracks. Tommy followed his gaze, and saw that he was staring at a blue-grey Siamese cat which was busily engaged in licking out an empty tin can, which lay in the vicinity of a row of dustbins, at the rear of the gymnasium.

'What a marvellous specimen of a Siamese cat,' Odell remarked to a small boy who was passing by at that moment. 'Who does it belong to?'

'That's Felix, sir!' The boy was obviously greatly honoured at being spoken to by the famous detective. 'It belongs to Mr. Norton.'

Richmond was eagerly awaiting their return. He seemed to sense that Odell was on the trail of something.

'I would like you to summon Woods and Norton down here at once,' Raymond Odell told him. 'I should also advise you to have a couple of your uniformed men in attendance. I am going to unmask the murderer of Walters, the headmaster, for you. I warn you, however, that it may come as quite a shock to everyone.'

It was a tense group of people who were gathered in the school library that evening, just as dusk was falling.

Richmond stood by the large latticed window, accompanied by Tommy Bourne. Two uniformed constables leaned on either doorpost, and seated on the edge of the table, in the centre of the room, for all the world like criminals facing a jury, were Patrick Norton, and Ted Woods. Raymond Odell stood in front of the huge fireplace, lighting his well-worn briar pipe.

'I have called you together,' he said, when it was drawing to his satisfaction, 'in order that we may clear this business up, once and for all, and destroy this atmosphere of guilt and suspicion which predominates at the moment. Now, Ted Woods, at 11.00 p.m. on Thursday last, you were engaged on some very nefarious activities.'

'It's a lie!' the janitor shouted, coming to his feet. 'I never done the old devil in, much as I've liked to 'ave done.'

'Nobody said you did,' Odell replied, never for one moment allowing the other's outburst to upset his self-control. 'As a matter of fact you were too busy poaching at the time, to worry about your headmaster. I picked a pheasant feather up off your floor this afternoon.'

Ted Woods subsided with a look of combined guilt and relief.

Odell continued, 'However, I'm not concerned with your poaching, even though I despise you for it. But you, Patrick Norton, murdered Walters, stole the staff wages, and attempted to throw the blame on to Woods.'

Norton jumped to his feet, looking as though he was going to risk running for it, but when he saw Detective-Inspector Richmond, and the two constables closing in on him, he changed his mind.

'Prove it!' he shouted. 'If you're so darned clever, Mr. Raymond Odell, prove it!'

'Alright,' smiled Odell, 'I'll do just that. On Thursday night, before you murdered Walters, you rang through to the Lodge, firstly to ascertain whether Woods had gone poaching, which you knew about, and therefore he would have no alibi, and secondly to establish an alibi for yourself with Mrs. Woods, by letting her know you were at your house. You had no intention of murder, only of stealing the wages. I have not yet established whether you are in financial difficulties or the theft was merely greed. Anyway, you found the French windows of Walters' study open. He was working there, and you stood in the curtains, watching on the off chance that he might leave the room, and give you your chance. Instead, however, he discovered your presence there, and in a moment of panic you hit him with one of a pair of Indian clubs which were close at hand. You were wearing gloves anyway, for fear of any prints you might leave behind whilst taking the money. Woods, being under suspicion of pilfering, was an ideal scapegoat for you.'

'You're guessing!' Norton now seemed very uncertain of himself.

'No, I'm not,' smiled Odell. 'Firstly, you left some tiny particles of slate on the lino on the headmaster's floor. There could only be one explanation where they came from, and that is from the slate path leading to your front door. Secondly, your Siamese cat is in the habit of sitting on your shoulder. Well, a hair from your cat rubbed off your shoulder on to the curtains in the murder room. It fooled me for a time, and, unknown to you, aided your scheme to incriminate Woods, for it wasn't until just now that I realised it was a cat's hair. Seeing your cat in the school grounds made me think twice about the hair I found on the curtains. Well, I examined the one from the curtain under a microscope in the school laboratories, and it confirmed my suspicion. Up until then I had half considered the possibility of a short, grey-haired man being the murderer.

'It seems that Felix, your faithful animal friend, has betrayed you Norton!'

Guy N. Smith

The Curse Of The Crystal

'I beg of you to come up to Leeds as quickly as you can, Mr. Odell.' There was genuine desperation in the voice of the middle-aged, grey-haired, little man with the goatee beard

Guy N. Smith

The Curse of the Crystal

'I beg of you to come up to Leeds as quickly as you can, Mr. Odell.' There was genuine desperation in the voice of the middle-aged, grey-haired, little man with the goatee beard, as he faced Raymond Odell, the famous detective, in the Dover Street consulting room. 'Unless you can come before midnight tomorrow night my father will die.'

Raymond Odell looked keenly at Reginald Mortimer, a building contractor from Yorkshire, who brought him such a strange request. He carefully filled and lighted his pipe before replying. Either the man was in desperate trouble, or else he was mad. Tommy Bourne, his young assistant, seated at the other end of the table, had already opened his notebook preparatory to writing.

'Don't you think you'd better start at the beginning and tell me the full story?' the Dover Street detective said. 'Once I have all the facts before me, I shall be in a position to give you an opinion.'

The man made an effort to pull himself together and began his story. 'All his life, Mr. Odell,' he said, 'my father has been a keen follower of the occult. He is 88 years of age, and apart from the usual ailments of the aged, is in fairly good health. He is always picking up some follower of the occult, and up to now it has done him no harm. Three weeks ago however, he met with this man Rattain. Rattain is a crystal-gazer and has pulled off one or two amazing predictions which has made him the last word with father. Father is a wealthy man and was undecided whether or not to sell some South American rubber shares which were slumping. Marlin, the family solicitor, pressed father to get rid of them for what they were worth whilst they were still saleable, but Rattain's crystal told him that they were going to soar by leaps and bounds. He was right! The following day they went up by nearly half. However, the day before yesterday this 'magician' let it out, by accident, he swears, that father is going to die of heart failure on the 20th, which is tomorrow, at midnight. Father has already resigned himself to it. He is willing himself to die, Mr. Odell!'

'Hmm,' said Odell, thoughtfully, 'there is mischief afoot somewhere. Has your father made a will in favour of this crystal gazer?'

'No,' Reggie Mortimer replied. 'I am absolutely certain that he has not.'

'Then I will be at your father's house at Leeds tomorrow morning,' Odell stated. 'Foul play is planned somehow, I am sure, and I will do my best to solve the mystery in time Mr. Mortimer.'

The Mortimer house was constructed of drab Yorkshire stone which was sorely in need of a clean. It had a general appearance of neglect, standing in its own grounds, which were choked with weeds. Raymond Odell rang the front doorbell and seconds later it was opened by Reggie Mortimer himself.

'I'll take you straight up to father's bedroom,' he said. 'He's already confined himself to bed. Marlin, our solicitor, is up there with him now.'

It was a very old, wizened, bald-headed man who looked up from the bedclothes as the detectives were shown in. Sitting by the bedside was a tall, dark man, with a pallid complexion.

'I'm glad you've come, Mr. Odell,' Marlin stated, in a flat, cold voice. 'Perhaps you can talk some sense into him and tell him he's not going to die.'

'You can't avoid fate,' the old man croaked. 'Nothing you can do will stop me dying at midnight tonight.'

Realizing the futility of trying to reason with Mortimer senior, Raymond Odell and Tommy Bourne followed the solicitor downstairs to the living room, where Reggie Mortimer's wife had made a pot of tea.

'I think,' the Dover Street detective stated, 'that the best thing for me to do would be to go and have a talk with this crystal-gazer, Rattain. If one of you would be good enough to supply me with his address, I will start at once.'

'I have it here, Mr. Odell,' Marlin replied, handing the detective a slip of paper, on which was written the address of an abode in a far from select quarter of the city. 'I must be on my way back to the office, though, as I have other work to attend to. Might I suggest that we all meet here at eleven o'clock tonight? I somehow think it would be a comfort to Mr. Mortimer, at least, if he had a few of his friends round him.'

Rattain himself answered the door to Raymond Odell's knock. He was a swarthy individual, dressed in Romany style, and decorated with earrings and charms.

'Come in, Mr. Raymond Odell,' he said. 'I was expecting you!'

Tommy Bourne had an uneasy feeling in his stomach as they followed the fortune-teller into a dimly lit room, hung with black tapestries, and decorated with the signs of the zodiac. Odell ignored his opening remark, determined to show the man that he was neither impressed nor frightened of him.

'I've got a severe warning for you, Rattain!' the Dover Street detective's voice cut through the air with venom. 'Call off this hocus-pocus on Mortimer, at once!'

'But I cannot alter fate, Mr. Odell I.....'

'Rubbish!' snarled Raymond Odell. 'If Mortimer dies, you're responsible, and you'll be in jail for your breakfast tomorrow!'

The detective wheeled round, and left by the front door, followed by Tommy Bourne.

'Gosh, guvnor,' said Tommy as they climbed back into their powerful car. 'We didn't get much change out of that.'

'On the contrary, Tommy,' replied Odell, 'I learnt what I came here for. Rattain is just a pawn in this game. I've frightened him badly, but now I need a further chat with Reginald Mortimer. We are racing against time.'

'Back already, Mr. Odell!' Reginald Mortimer seemed surprised to see the detectives again so soon.

'I just want a scrap of information from you,' the detective snapped. 'On what day did Rattain forecast the rise of your father's rubber shares in South America?'

The other scratched his head in bewilderment and thought hard for a couple of minutes. 'I remember,' he said. 'It was last Wednesday, the 13th.'

'Right,' snapped Odell. 'I've got a lot of work to do between now and midnight, and I only hope I can prove what I think. I'm going to leave Tommy with you, as a precautionary measure, in case I am not successful. I want him to discreetly put all the clocks in the house back by an hour, unknown to your father. If the worst comes to the worst, and we can get him through midnight, and then tell him he's lived past zero hour, it might do the trick. We are up against a deadly psychological murderer. I pray that I shall be in time!'

It was a tense atmosphere in the Mortimer bedroom that night at 10.30 p.m. The old man lay back with his eyes closed, having already resigned himself to his fate. Reggie Mortimer and his wife sat on either side of the bed. Marlin, the solicitor, was in the easy chair by the window, and Tommy Bourne occupied a straight-backed chair near to the door. Nobody spoke.

Tommy wondered how his chief was getting on. The minutes were ticking away fast, but he knew that it was not like the Dover Street detective to waste time. Somewhere, somehow, he was working in an effort to beat the clock.

The clock on the mantleshelf showed that it was now half-past ten. Actually, the real time was half-past eleven, for the young detective had put back all the clocks in the house back an hour, as instructed.

'Mr. Odell, seems to be taking his time.' There was a note of sarcasm in the lawyer's voice. Tommy was about to provide him with a suitable reply when he heard a car coming up the drive below, followed a couple of minutes later by footsteps on the stairs. The bedroom door opened, and in walked Raymond Odell, followed by a burly police inspector, and a constable.

'Well, Mr. Odell,' said Reggie Mortimer, 'have you had any luck?'

'I have,' replied the Dover Street detective. 'Rattain has been arrested, and now I am about to land the big fish!'

He paused, and then he turned his gaze onto the pallid features of Marlin, the solicitor. 'Arrest that man, Inspector!' he snapped. 'I think we've arrived just in time.'

The solicitor's countenance became even paler, and he made no attempt to resist as the constable stepped forward, putting the hand-cuffs on him, whilst the inspector charged him. 'I don't quite understand, Mr. Odell' said Reggie Mortimer. 'Are you sure you've got the right man?'

'Absolutely!' replied Raymond Odell. 'I knew Rattain was a fake, and also that he was merely working for someone else. The fact that he was aware that I was visiting him this afternoon was not evidence of the powers of his crystal. Someone had warned him in advance, and I knew that warning could only have come from this household. The question was being able to prove it. I decided that the best line of attack was through his earlier predictions. I decided to work on the one in which he forecast the rise of the South American rubber shares. You told me that your father had not made a will in favour of Rattain, but you omitted to tell me that he had been persuaded to leave his solicitor two thousand pounds. Quite a normal thing. Many clients who feel themselves indebted to their lawyers leave them something. Well, Marlin was in dire financial difficulties. He had embezzled another client for a thousand pounds and was in danger of being found out. He desperately needed the money to replace what he had taken. So he hit upon this plan of murdering Mr. Mortimer senior, in a way that would leave absolutely no trace. Rattain has made a full confession that will be sufficient to put Marlin away for a very long time. I persuaded the GPO to trace the telegram which I suspected must have been sent to Marlin, from South America, the day previous to Rattain telling Mr. Mortimer that his shares would go up. As Merlin had full control of his affairs, it was a reasonable supposition that it was he who would have been advised. The GPO were most helpful and succeeded in turning up a copy of the telegram. Marlin received it on the 12th, Rattain made his prediction on the 13th!'

The old man had opened his eyes, and now he was struggling up into a sitting position.

'He'll be OK in a day or two,' Reggie said, 'you've saved his life Mr. Odell. By the way, I thought that was a brilliant idea of yours about putting the clocks back an hour.'

Raymond Odell shook his head. 'It wouldn't have been good enough,' he said. 'I slipped up. I completely forgot about the church clock across the road. Its midnight chimes would have been sufficient to kill your father. Fortunately, I managed to obtain the evidence I wanted, and get back here in time.'

Death On The Stairs

Hugh Masters had been drinking again. His beautiful wife Vera knew this for a certainty as the unmelodious strains of his voice reached her from the landing above, as she stood in the hall of their large country house, clad in evening dress, waiting for him.

Guy N. Smith

Death on the Stairs

Hugh Masters had been drinking again. His beautiful wife Vera knew this for a certainty as the unmelodious strains of his voice reached her from the landing above, as she stood in the hall of their large country house, clad in evening dress, waiting for him. She sighed, for she envisaged another embarrassing evening at the dinner which they were due to attend.

Suddenly he appeared at the top of the stairs, an inane grin on his face as he continued to sing, twirling a short cane in his right hand. His wife watched as he endeavoured to negotiate the stairs, holding on to the bannister with one hand for support, as each step presented an obstacle to him. She gave a gasp as he appeared to slip, and next second he was falling headlong to land in an ungainly heap in the hall below. She ran to him, expecting a broken limb at the very worst, and then she saw it.... a knife protruding from the right hand side of his neck!

A couple of hours later Raymond Odell, the famous Dover Street detective, and his assistant, Tommy Bourne, arrived at Wycliffe House the home of the late Hugh Masters, in answer to a summons from their official colleague, Detective-Inspector Richmond of Scotland Yard. Richmond opened the door to admit them himself. The body still lay in the hall, and a group of fingerprint experts were already at work.

'Glad you got here, Odell,' Richmond greeted them. 'Though it now seems you won't be needed. I'm almost on the verge of arresting Ricci Verranti, Hugh Masters' secretary.'

'I may as well have a look round as I've taken the trouble to come down,' Odell replied, and patiently waited until the fingerprint experts had finished before beginning his own investigations.

He began with an examination of the body, using his powerful lens in order that he might detect something which the naked eye had missed.

'Ah!' a sudden exclamation escaped his lips, and he turned to Richmond and Tommy, holding up a length of thread which he had found entwined round the dead man's cane. 'Now where did this come from? He's wearing no clothing of this material.'

He worked for another ten minutes without finding anything further, and then, followed by Tommy, he let himself in to the drawing room where Richmond was busy interviewing Vera Masters.

'I tell you, inspector,' she almost pleaded, 'I saw him fall with my own eyes. Ricci was in the library adjoining the landing, I know, but in no way could he possibly have been responsible for Hugh's death.'

'You don't seem exactly heartbroken over your husband's death.' It was a statement rather than a question. Vera Masters paled but did not reply.

Raymond Odell went back into the hall, and eventually he was joined by Richmond.

'I've just had a report from the fingerprint men,' the Yard man said. 'There's no doubt about it, Verranti's fingerprints are on the murder weapon. I guess I can go right ahead and arrest him now.'

'Just hold on for a bit,' Raymond Odell advised. 'I'm not too happy about this case just at the moment. Now, Ricci Verranti was in the library adjoining the landing. Mrs. Masters stood in the hall. A knife appears from nowhere and strikes down Hugh Masters. Either they are both lying, or else there's something very sinister about the whole affair.'

'Look guvnor!' Tommy Bourne was pointing to a small window, almost at the top of the stairs. 'That's where the blue thread came from. Off that silk tassel on the end of that cord on the window!'

'I do believe you're right, Tommy,' snapped Raymond Odell. 'Now, Richmond, I'd appreciate it if I could have a few words with this Ricci Verranti.'

The Yard man motioned for them to follow him into the library, where the secretary sat slumped in a chair, his head in his hands. He looked up as they entered, and Odell saw that he was a very handsome man, in his mid-thirties, but with the swarthiness of a foreigner.

'Yes, I handled the knife only yesterday,' he replied in answer to the Dover Street detective's question. 'Mr. Masters asked me to bring it to him so that he could slit some letters open. He said he was unable to find the paper-knife.'

'I see,' Raymond Odell was lighting his pipe as he spoke, 'how did you get on with Hugh Masters?'

'I hated him,' the reply was venomous.

'But you did not hate Mrs. Masters,' Odell saw the secretary start as he delivered this last bombshell, and realised that this insinuation, a shot in the dark, had found its target. Verranti did not reply.

A few minutes later Raymond Odell was again conducting a thorough search, this time in the area of the small window with the fancy cord.

'Look, Richmond!' he suddenly cried, pointing to something that rested behind the curtains. 'That's the answer to our problem. What a devilish contraption!'

Richmond and Tommy Bourne looked where the Dover Street detective was pointing. Screwed into the window frame, partly hidden by the curtains, was something that resembled a miniature crossbow, about six inches in length. 'It looks like a small crossbow,' snapped Richmond.

'That's exactly what it is,' Raymond Odell replied. 'Only instead of firing a bolt, it fired the knife that killed Masters. Find me a screwdriver, Tommy, and we'll get it down. Then I should like to have another chat with Vera Masters and Ricci Verranti.'

Ten minutes later, the two Dover Street detectives, and Detective-Inspector Richmond faced Vera Masters and Ricci Verranti across the drawing room table. The ingenious knife-throwing device rested in front of them.

'Now,' began Raymond Odell, 'let's tackle the remaining problems. Firstly, Mrs. Masters, were you and Ricci Verranti having an affair?'

The lady of the house coloured slightly, before replying with a rather hesitant, 'Yes.'

'Well,' said Odell, 'at least there's a motive for the crime then.'

'What d'you mean?' snarled Verranti, a flush appearing on his swarthy face.

'I'll explain,' Raymond Odell was completely unperturbed by the other's outburst. 'Now, we've established that there was an affair going on between Mrs. Masters and Ricci Verranti. Hugh Masters must have been aware of this, in a small household such as this, and he planned a very terrible revenge. He invented and installed this miniature crossbow on the landing window, operated by the pull-cord. Firstly, he had to have Ricci Verranti's fingerprints on the knife, and this was easily obtained by asking his secretary to fetch it from the collection for use as a paper-knife. He took care not to get his own prints on it, and fixed it ready for use. Now, Mr. Verranti, did he at any time request that you personally saw to the closing of the windows at night?'

'He did, indeed, Mr. Odell,' Ricci Verranti replied. 'He has insisted for the past fortnight that I made it my own personal duty to ensure that the windows were closed at night, particularly the landing one which he said was very vulnerable to burglars.'

'Ah,' mused Odell. 'The pieces of this jigsaw begin to fit together. Having ensured that it would be you who would pull the blind, and trigger off this diabolical weapon, he put his plan into action. You would have been dead by now, Mr. Verranti, had not Hugh Masters become drunk, and in a state of intoxication set off his own devilish device by accidentally catching it with his cane.'

'It all sounds very well, Odell,' put in the matter-of-fact Richmond. 'But don't you think we are working too much on theories without facts to back them up. After all, it could have been either Mr. Verranti or Mrs. Masters, for all we know, who rigged up the booby trap, and succeeded in killing Hugh Masters.'

Raymond Odell smiled and shook his head. 'No Richmond,' he replied. 'Only Hugh Masters knew about this little device. Had it been anybody else, they would have had the time, and the opportunity, to remove it before the police were called in. It was not removed, because nobody living knew that it was there. The villain who thought it all up has perished by his own trickery.'

Dressed To Kill

Raymond Odell, the famous Dover Street detective, and his young assistant, Tommy Bourne, were enjoying a short holiday in the country. They had booked in at the Feathers Hotel, a quiet country residence, set in the heart of Herefordshire

Guy N. Smith

Dressed to Kill

Raymond Odell, the famous Dover Street detective, and his young assistant, Tommy Bourne, were enjoying a short holiday in the country. They had booked in at the Feathers Hotel, a quiet country residence, set in the heart of Herefordshire, and were spending a few days just concentrating on golf, and the odd long walk.

It was during dinner on their first evening that they became acquainted with Lionel Ratcliffe. He was the one permanent guest in the small hotel, and he was quite the most unpleasant character it had been their misfortune to meet in a long time. He was a thin-faced, bespectacled man in his late fifties, and it was quite obvious to the handful of diners that the kitchen staff and waiters were frightened of him. He openly criticised the food and service, creating a distinct tension in the small dining room.

'Just listen to that fellow in the corner, guvnor!' Tommy Bourne remarked, before they had finished their second course. 'I wonder they don't throw him out!'

'Yes, he does seem to have a decidedly bad temper,' was the only remark Odell made.

Odell and Tommy shared a room on the third floor of the building, the only two other rooms on that floor being a bedroom opposite, occupied by none other than Lionel Ratcliffe himself, and a bathroom at the far end of the corridor. They could use either the main flight of stairs, or a small, winding staircase which led to the ground floor via the servants' quarters.

They returned to the hotel shortly before six o'clock on the second day of their stay, after a tiring day on the local golf course. Dinner was not served until 7.30 p.m., so they had ample time to change.

It was while they were in the midst of changing, at about 6.20, that there was a sudden flash, and the whole of their floor was plunged into darkness.

'A fuse has gone I expect,' remarked Odell, as he found a candle that he had placed on the dressing room table to cater for emergencies such as this, and lit it. However, within a space of three minutes, the lights had come on again, and with some relief Tommy blew out the naked flame.

It was almost 7.15 before they were ready to descend to the dining room on the ground floor, and just as they were preparing to leave their room, they heard a loud thud from somewhere on the floor below them. Noises such as this are not uncommon in hotels, and so they thought no more about it until they reached the stairs. There, below them, lying in a heap on the landing of the second floor, was the body of a man. They had no difficulty in recognising the plus-four clad figure as that of the ill-mannered Lionel Ratcliffe.

Raymond Odell was at his side in a second, but he knew the moment that he tried to lift the man into a sitting position that there was nothing anybody could do for him. He was dead.

'It is certainly fortunate for us that you happened to be staying at the Feathers, Mr. Odell,' said Inspector Rowan of the local constabulary, on the following day, as he sipped his pint of beer with Odell and Tommy in a secluded corner of the residents' lounge. 'There's something very peculiar about this Ratcliffe business. When the proprietor, Frank Bennett, telephoned us last night, I was inclined to dismiss the matter as natural causes, or perhaps misadventure. However, there is absolutely *nothing* to show how this man died! The postmortem this afternoon showed that he was a perfectly normal, healthy individual. There weren't even any bones broken by his fall on the stairs. It is a queer business, take it from me.'

'I'll make one or two enquiries for you, if you like,' Odell replied. 'Actually, Tommy and I are on holiday, but we don't mind lending you a hand if we can be any help.'

'I'd be most grateful,' Inspector Rowan sighed, with a hint of relief.

It transpired when Raymond Odell began questioning the hotel staff that the general porter/handyman, Bill Reeves, a retired army sergeant, had seen Ratcliffe on his way to the bathroom, as was his daily routine, just before 6 p.m., clad in dressing gown and slippers.

'Was he a tidy man, generally?' Odell asked.

'Exceedingly so, sir,' was the reply. 'His was the tidiest bedroom in the whole hotel - even if he was the most unpleasant guest that we've ever had staying here!'

'And yet the towel and flannel were just flung on the floor of the bathroom after he'd finished bathing,' mused Odell. 'Did he always change for dinner?'

'Always' said Reeves. 'He was very fussy.'

The following morning, after breakfast, Odell, aided by Tommy, began a minute inspection of the third floor bathroom. It was a large room, incorporating a full size bath and large linen cupboard, which the proprietor, Frank Bennett, informed them was never used, due to the fact that steam from the bath dampened anything that was stored in it. It was quite superfluous. 'And dusty too,' Odell commented. 'Just a minute...' He dropped to his hands and knees, and began to examine the floor of the small compartment with the aid of his powerful magnifying lens. 'Somebody's been standing in here, and recently too. Look Tommy, you can see the footmarks in the dust.'

Tommy Bourne looked and saw that his chief was indeed right. But Raymond Odell was moving on, like a bloodhound that had located a scent. 'Where's the heater gone?' He was talking as much to himself as he was to Tommy. 'It was in here the first night we arrived. I know, because I used it. An old-fashioned single-bar electric type. The fitting's here by the washstand, but where the dickens has the heater, flex and plug gone?'

Frank Bennett, the hotel proprietor, was a thickset man in his late forties. He reminded Odell of an owl, as he peered across the desk of his office at the two Dover Street detectives.

'Tell me,' Raymond Odell began. 'where are the various members of your hotel staff situated between 6 and 6.30 p.m. under normal circumstances?'

'There is usually hardly anybody available at that time,' Bennett replied. 'It is a busy time, prior to dinner. The dining-room staff are busy changing, and the kitchen staff are preparing the meal. I am probably the only one on duty to answer queries, and any other little job that might crop up. I usually remain in the reception until about 7.30 p.m.'

'I see,' Odell replied. 'Who, then, replaced the fuse in the fusebox on the third floor, when the lights failed the other evening?'

'I did,' the proprietor replied.

'Then you were very quick about it. It was completed in a matter of three minutes flat. You must hold the record for mending fuses, Mr. Bennett, to manage to mount the stairs to the third floor, find a spare fuse, by the aid of torchlight, and fit it inside that time. But the real question is- how did you know the lights on our landing had failed? They cannot be seen from here!'

'Mr. Ratcliffe fetched me.'

'He was in the bath at that time, I believe,' Odell read from his notes. 'You killed Lionel Ratcliffe, Mr. Bennett, and I'll tell you how you did it.'

The hotel proprietor sank his head into his hands and leaned forward on the desk. For a few seconds, he remained thus, and then he looked up, and met Odell's steely gaze.

'You're right, Mr. Odell,' he sighed. 'But I should be interested to hear your deductions.'

'I presume,' the Dover Street detective began, lighting his battered briar pipe, 'that Lionel Ratcliffe had some hold over you, otherwise you would not have tolerated the way he behaved towards you and your staff. You had obviously had as much as you could stand of him, so, knowing his daily routine, you planned to kill him in a way which, if you were lucky, would leave no trace. You knew what time he would take his daily bath, so you hid in the large cupboard in the bathroom. No doubt we shall be able to prove that the footprints in the dust are yours. You waited until he was in the bath, and then you switched on the electric fire, and dropped it into the bath with him. Naturally, it fused the lights as well as killing him. Under cover of the sudden darkness, you dragged him back to his bedroom. You took his dressing gown and slippers with you, but left the bathroom in an untidy state, which was quite out of character, as far as he was concerned. You removed the heater, and then quickly replaced the fuse in the fusebox, putting all the lights back on again. You then dressed him, in his plus-fours, and dropped him down the front stairs, making your own retreat down the rear ones. You were then able to appear in the reception as though you had been there all the time. Your mistakes were that you did not dress him up in his lounge suit, which would have appeared feasible and that by tying his tie from the front, you made it appear as if it had been tied by a left-handed man. Only a man with an intimate knowledge of the hotel, and of the guest in question, would have been able to do all this. With all the staff fully employed at the time, you would not be missed for the hour that you spent in Ratcliffe's bedroom setting up this 'accident'. Indeed, only you would have had the opportunity to do all the things I have mentioned.'

'You must have supernatural powers, Mr. Odell,' whispered Frank Bennett. 'Lionel Ratcliffe was blackmailing me over an incident in my earlier life. He has been living here free, for the past few months, and then when he began demanding money, that was the last straw, so I killed him!'

'I'd better contact Inspector Rowan.' Odell reached for the phone.

Concrete Evidence

'I'd appreciate your help in this business, Odell,' said Detective Inspector Richmond of the CID, seating himself in the comfortable armchair in the Dover Street detective's consulting room. 'One of our River Patrols fished a body out of the Thames last week

Guy N. Smith

Concrete Evidence

'I'd appreciate your help in this business, Odell,' said Detective Inspector Richmond of the CID, seating himself in the comfortable armchair in the Dover Street detective's consulting room. 'One of our River Patrols fished a body out of the Thames last week, whilst dragging for a suicide. It's taken us five days to identify the man.'

Raymond Odell, the famous detective, paused momentarily to light his battered briar pipe, signalling at the same time for his official colleague to continue with the story.

'The man had been shot in the back of the head at close range with a .38 revolver,' the Yard man went on. 'His feet had been encased in a block of concrete, and the tailor's tabs had been removed from his clothing. However, in the turn-ups of his trousers, we found gold dust, which indicated that he worked as a manufacturing jeweler. This narrowed our search down considerably, and we eventually discovered that he was William Walton, the senior partner in the Walton Jewelry Company, with his nephew, John Walton, a young man of about twenty-five years of age. William was a bachelor in his late fifties. He had been missing since Tuesday night, but it was quite usual for him to go off for days at a time on his own, without saying anything to anybody, so nobody had thought his absence strange. It is only a small business, the two Waltons, a man of about thirty-five named Rainbow who cuts and fits all the stones for them, and a middle-aged spinster, Mildred James, who looks after the small retail shop on the premises. In other words, it's a typical small family firm. There is no apparent motive for the murder. It seems that William Walton did not have an enemy in the world!'

'Tell,' Odell commented, rising to his feet, 'the obvious thing for me to do is to interview John Walton, Mildred James, and Rainbow. I'll ask Tommy to bring the car round now, if that's all right with you?'

'Fine,' Richmond replied. 'The sooner we start, the better. I'll just give John Walton a ring and let him know we're coming round.'

An hour later, Raymond Odell, followed by Tommy Bourne, his young assistant, and Detective Inspector Richmond, entered the premises of the Walton Jewellery Company. The shop was empty of customers, and a woman with streaks of grey in her raven black hair, looked at them with red-rimmed eyes. This could be none other than Mildred James.

'Mr. Walton, junior, is expecting you' she stated, expressionlessly. 'Please go straight through the workshop, and through the blue door at the far end.'

They did as instructed, and as they crossed the floor of the workshop, they noticed a dark-haired man with a handsome pale face, bending over a bench, so engrossed in his work that he never even noticed their presence.

John Walton rose from behind his desk as they entered his office and greeted them cordially.

'A terrible business, this,' he attempted to smile, and brushed his unruly red hair back from his forehead with one hand.

'This is Mr. Raymond Odell, the private investigator.' Richmond seemed rather abrupt. 'I'd like him to interview the staff here.' Perhaps you wouldn't mind starting the ball rolling, Mr. Walton?'

'Certainly,' the other replied. 'When you've finished with me, Mr. Odell, I'll step outside, and you can use my office to question Miss James and Mr. Rainbow.'

'I take it you are now the sole owner of the Walton Jewellery Company?' Raymond Odell began.

'That is so.'

'How did you get on with your uncle?'

'Not particularly well,' Walton replied. 'We had a permanent difference of opinion. He lived in the past, and absolutely refused to move with the times. The business could have expanded to twice its present size if I'd had my way.'

'And privately?'

'We never saw each other outside of business hours. He was a total recluse!'

Charles Rainbow had a negative personality and apart from his wife and young son, had no interest outside his work. He worked conscientiously and had neither liked nor disliked William Walton. Raymond Odell found him very much of a bore, and was relieved to see Mildred James come in.

'You seem much more upset over this business than I would have expected, even from the most devoted employee,' the Dover Street detective commented, as the tear-stained shop assistant looked at him across the desk.

'I was more than just the shop-girl here, Mr. Odell,' she fought to control her sobs. 'You see... I was engaged to marry William Walton!'

Raymond Odell gave no sign of the surprise he felt.

'Nobody knew about this up until a fortnight or so ago,' she went on. 'Then John found out. He was simply furious. It was the old story of the family business having to be split three ways instead of two, and he sulked and brooded for days.'

'Weren't you worried about William Walton's disappearance over these past few days?'

Mildred James shook her head.

'Not really,' she replied. 'It was quite usual for him to go away on business for a few days, or else to take a well-earned holiday aboard his nephew's boat on the Thames.'

'John Walton has a boat!' Odell gripped the edge of the desk until his knuckles showed white.

'Oh yes,' the other replied. 'Didn't he tell you? It's a river cruiser called the 'Narita'. It's his hobby, his sole interest in life.'

'Can you give me the exact location of its mooring?' the Dover Street detective tried to keep the excitement out of his voice.

'Oh yes,' Mildred James replied. 'I know exactly where John Walton keeps his boat!'

The late afternoon sunshine was glistening on a quiet autumnal riverside scene, as Raymond Odell, Tommy Bourne and Richmond walked the hundred yards or so from the parked car to this backwater of the River Thames, where a gaily painted motor-yacht, bearing the name 'The Narita' floated at its moorings. There was no sign of anybody about, so it was a simple matter for them to step on board the craft. The cabin door was locked, but this was no real obstacle to a man of Odell's ability, and after a few minutes probing with a small instrument which he produced from his pocket, there was a 'click' and the door swung open. The detective entered the small cabin and began pulling open locker drawers.

'Ah!' he exclaimed at last, holding up a navy blue polo-necked sweater. There was a reddish-brown stain on the front of it, and what looked like particles of human hair adhered to it. 'This blood and hair have come from the dead man,' the detective murmured to himself. 'No doubt this happened when the murderer threw his victim overboard.'

'We'd better get back and arrest John Walton.' Detective Inspector Richmond was always inclined to be direct in his methods.

'Not so fast,' said Odell, beginning to fill his pipe. 'There's more to this than meets the eye.'

He held up something in his hand, which sparkled and scintillated in the rays of the dying sun. Richmond and Tommy peered at it, and the young detective emitted a whistle of surprise.

'It's a ruby!' he gasped.

'Correct,' Odell replied. 'But not just an ordinary ruby. You can see how it has been cut to a peculiar shape. Well, that has been done to disguise its original shape. I have no doubt whatsoever that it is a well known stone that has been stolen and re-cut. It loses value of course, but that is better for the thief than having a valuable article which he can't sell.'

'I'm still not quite clear on the present situation,' declared Richmond, scratching the back of his head.

'Nor am I, altogether,' replied Odell. 'It does rather seem a bit of a mix up. The senior partner of a family business is found dead at the bottom of a river. His nephew, the other partner, has quarreled with him over his intended marriage to the shop assistant. The nephew tries to hide the fact that he owns a boat on the Thames, close to where his uncle's body was found. We find this out from a third party, and on investigating the craft, we discover a blood-stained sweater, with hairs which undoubtedly come from the dead man adhering to it. We also find a ruby which has been re-cut. So, somewhere along the line, jewel thieves are involved.'

'We'd better arrest John Walton!' Richmond's thoughts were still channelled in this direction.

'Not just at the moment,' Odell replied calmly. 'There's one more line which we haven't investigated. The murdered man's feet had been encased in concrete in order to keep the body on the bottom of the river. Now, ordinary cement takes some time to set particularly if it has to be submerged in water. There is a new kind of 'waterproof' quick-drying cement that has only recently been advertised on commercial television. From what you tell me, Richmond, this is the stuff that was used to weight William Walton's body. Sales of this brand are sure to be limited at the start, so I suggest that the three of us split up, and check out every shop that sells 'Conset' within a radius of a mile or so of the Walton Jewellery Company.

There's just a chance that they might be able to give us a description of the killer. We'll make a start right away. It'll be another hour yet before the shops close.'

Mildred James was on the point of shutting and bolting the shop door when Raymond Odell, Tommy and Richmond stepped over the threshold.

'You're just in time, gentlemen,' she said. 'Mr. Walton is still in his office. You know the way...'

With a brief nod, Odell, followed by the other two, crossed the retail shop, and entered the workshop.

Charles Rainbow glanced up as they came in.

'Mr. Rainbow,' Raymond Odell paused; seemingly as an afterthought, 'I wonder if you could tell me, approximately, the cost of cutting this stone!' As he spoke, the detective tossed the ruby, which he had found onboard the 'Narita' on the workbench. Rainbow recalled in alarm.

'Where... where... did you get that?'

'I picked it up where you dropped it, onboard John Walton's yacht where you murdered William Walton,' replied Odell. 'I also found John Walton's sweater, stained with blood, which you wore to commit the crime, thinking to throw the blame on your boss!'

Rainbow glanced round in panic, seeking a way of escape, but Detective Inspector Richmond had already placed a hand on his shoulder.

'Don't try it son,' he warned. 'You wouldn't get far.'

Charles Rainbow sat down on the chair behind him and sank his head in his hands.

'I'll confess,' he sobbed. 'I just want to get it off my chest. I'd been re-cutting valuable stones for a gang of jewel thieves and William Walton found out about me. He was going to shop me, I know, and he went and stayed on his nephew's boat as he was wont to do when he had a problem on his mind. I killed him there. I knew I'd lost that ruby somewhere, but I daren't go back to the 'Narita' to look for it. But how did you get on to me anyway?'

'It was the 'Conset' which gave you away,' Raymond Odell replied. 'The assistant in the hardware and building supplies shop next-door-but-one remembers selling you a 7 lb bag of it. You hoped to throw the blame on John Walton, but I'm glad to say your plan misfired. No doubt the revolver with which you shot Walton senior is at the bottom of the Thames, but I'm sure its recovery won't be necessary to prove your guilt!'

Quick-Change Artist

'I'm glad I found you free this afternoon, Odell,' Detective Inspector Richmond said as the police car sped through the London traffic. Tommy Bourne, Odell's young assistant, sat in the back with his famous chief. He had no idea where they were going, or what was afoot

Guy N. Smith

Quick-Change Artist

'I'm glad I found you free this afternoon, Odell,' Detective Inspector Richmond said as the police car sped through the London traffic. Tommy Bourne, Odell's young assistant, sat in the back with his famous chief. He had no idea where they were going, or what was afoot, but he always appreciated these sudden appearances of the Yard man. They heralded excitement.

'There's been a murder,' Richmond went on. 'I was down there all morning. The body's been taken away by now, and the photographers and fingerprint men have done their work, so you can nose around without any fear of spoiling any evidence. It's the old story of a meek and mild husband, and a large, ferocious, bad-tempered wife. The wife was found dead this morning, her head staved in with an axe. A messy job, I can tell you! There's no sign of the husband, though - he's just vanished into thin air! The reason I asked you to come down with me is that there is not a single fingerprint of the husband's in the whole flat anywhere! Anyway, you can question the only two people who might know anything about him; the caretaker, and an artist fellow who lives in the flat immediately above.'

The flat in question was in a skyscraper block of thirty. The detective took the lift up to the ninth floor where they found a constable on duty outside the front door.

'This is where the body lay,' Richmond pointed to a blood-stained patch on the living room carpet. 'James Jenkinson has been nagged by his wife for the past twenty years. At last the worm turned. He smashed her head in with this little axe. But why on earth take the trouble to wipe the place clean of every fingerprint before doing a bunk? It just doesn't add up!'

'It doesn't,' Odell agreed. 'Anyway, I'd like to interview the other people you mentioned concerned in the case.'

'I'll get the constable on duty to call them,' Richmond replied. 'They both live on the premises. Robinson, the elderly caretaker is one, and the artist, John Parsons, who lives above this flat is the other.'

Robinson the caretaker was well into his seventies. A very respectful man, he had white hair and a white moustache. There were traces of snuff down the front of his shabby waistcoat.

'Yes, sir,' he said in reply to Raymond Odell's question. 'I've known the Jenkinsons ever since they moved into this flat five years ago. The wife knew them about fifteen years before that. Never been happy ever since they were married. She's made his life hell. Very often he used to come down and have a chat to me, merely to keep out of her way. Or else he'd go up to that shifty artist fellow who lived over their flat.'

'How old was he?' enquired Odell.

'Oh, I should say somewhere about forty-five,' replied Robinson. 'His wife hated this artist chap Parsons. If there'd been a row he would either come and spend an hour with myself or Parsons.'

'What do you know about Parsons?' the Dover Street detective asked.

'Very little,' the caretaker replied. 'In fact, I don't like the chap. He's been living here for about five years, same as the Jenkinsons. For days on end you'd never see him at all. His painting is all he lives for, and if anyone interrupted him in his work, he'd fly into a terrible rage. However, he seemed to get on well with Jenkinson, and would sometimes spend a whole day with him at weekends.'

'What did Jenkinson do for a living?' asked Odell.

The old man scratched his head. 'Some sort of representative, I think,' he said. 'Anyway, some days he didn't even bother going to work at all, and used to go up, and spend the day with Parsons.'

John Parsons was a typical bachelor-artist. His dress was bohemian, and his untidy hair fell below his shoulders in long greasy locks. He had thick-lensed, horn-rimmed spectacles, a goatee beard and moustache. He would have seemed more at home in Paris than in a luxury block in the West End of London.

'How long have you known Jenkinson?' asked Raymond Odell.

'Oh, about five years,' was the reply. 'I have seen more of him lately, though. His wife's nagging and tantrums have grown a hundred times worse this last six months. He'd come and spend an hour or two just watching me paint. He never used to say very much at all. Whenever he'd got a day off work he'd dress as though he was going to the office, and then come and spend the day upstairs with me. Personally, I liked the fellow.'

'Any idea where he might've gone?' the Dover Street detective asked.

The artist shook his head. 'No idea at all I'm afraid. He hadn't got many friends. I suppose he's just panicked and run.'

'You heard nothing unusual in the early hours of this morning, by any chance, did you, Mr. Parsons?' Odell asked.

The other shook his head.

'No,' he answered. 'I'm a very heavy sleeper. It would take an earthquake to wake me up.'

'Ever been in this flat before?' Odell's eyes were boring into him.

'Never,' was the reply. 'His wife hated the sight of me, probably because I was his refuge in stormy weather.'

'I see he's left a pile of business correspondence behind on the table,' Odell remarked. 'I'd better tie it into a bundle and take it away to go through at my leisure. I wonder if you'd be good enough to find me some string, Mr. Parsons.'

'Certainly,' replied Parsons, and crossing to the kitchen cupboard, he opened it, and reached down a ball of thick brown twine from the top shelf. 'Well, I'll be getting along, Mr. Odell. If you want me any more, I'll be in the flat above.'

Two days later found Detective Inspector Richmond seated in the Dover Street detective's consulting rooms.

'Well,' Richmond snapped. 'We haven't located Jenkinson yet. All the airports and seaports have been alerted, but he just seems to have vanished.'

'I thought he might.' Raymond Odell drew on his pipe. 'I don't think we shall pick him up just like that. However, I do have a little experiment in mind... ring up the artist, Parsons, and get him down to the Yard for more routine questioning. Waste as much time as possible with him. I want you to give me time for a look round his flat.'

'You think he might be hiding Jenkinson up there?' The idea was clearly new to him.

'It's certainly a possibility,' admitted Raymond Odell with a laugh...

QUICK-CHANGE ARTIST

*   *   *

The late winter sunlight filtered through the wide windows as Odell and Tommy let themselves into Parsons' studio flat. They had watched the artist board a bus for Whitehall, and then entered the flat; the front door had offered little resistance.

The flat was set up as a studio, pictures, easels, paints etc. dominating the scene. The bed was unmade, and the place was thick with dust. It was obvious that it had not been cleaned properly during the entire time that Parsons had rented the place.

'Excellent!' exclaimed Odell, surveying the dusty scene. 'Stand here by the door, Tommy, and don't move about.'

Tommy Bourne did as his famous chief requested and stood watching him move about the flat. Every so often, Odell knelt down and measured a footprint in the dust.

'Size eight, every one of them!' he commented finally, pocketing his ruler. 'Get hold of Richmond and tell him to keep Parsons talking there at all costs till we arrive.'

*   *   *

John Parsons turned round in surprise as the door of Detective Inspector Richmond's office opened to admit Raymond Odell and Tommy Bourne.

'Why, Mr. Odell,' there was a trace of uneasiness in the artist's voice. 'Fancy seeing you here!'

'Hello, Odell,' Richmond remained seated behind the desk. 'Anything to report?'

'You could say that,' Raymond Odell replied. 'As a matter of fact, I've located the elusive James Jenkinson.'

'What!' Richmond leapt from his desk. 'Where is he? I'll have him arrested at once!'

'He's sitting in front of you. John Parsons and James Jenkinson are one and the same!'

A shocked silence settled over the room. The artist sunk his head in his hands and bowed forward.

'Would you like to make a confession, and make it easier for yourself?' Richmond asked. 'Or shall I get Mr. Odell to explain it all?'

'I'll tell you everything you want to know,' replied Jenkinson, pulling himself together. 'My life's been absolute hell from the very first day I married that woman. I put up with it for the first fifteen years, but when we moved into that flat, the flat above ours was also vacant, and I got the idea of renting it in the name of John Parsons, an artist who required only to be left in peace and was seldom seen. I had no close friends, so a disguise was fairly easy. My wife took a dislike to my artist friend on principle, without even seeing him, so that saved a lot of bother. A wig, and a false goatee beard and moustache and I had complete freedom to pursue my lifelong interest - painting. My wife would never allow so much as a paintbrush in our flat. The inevitable day came at last. I could stand her no longer, and we had a row in which I lost my temper for the first time in twenty years. During the heat of the argument, I picked up an axe and killed her! Then I hit upon what seemed a wonderful idea. I would not run like a common murderer. I would assume the identity of John Parsons, artist, for good.'

'It was certainly a clever idea,' Odell explained, 'and it stood a fair chance of success, but for your initial blunders. You told me you had never been in the murder flat before - yet you knew exactly where the string was kept! Then your efforts to remove all traces of Jenkinson by wiping the whole flat clear of fingerprints made me think; it was obviously an attempt to ensure you could not be traced, unnecessary if you were going far since your prints would be unlikely to be checked. Therefore you hadn't gone far. I decided to search your flat this afternoon, while you were detained here. Your other big mistake was not cleaning the place. The floor was thick with dust, and there were footprints all over the place. I checked the footprints. They were all size eight. Jenkinson was supposed to have visited regularly, and therefore there would have been slight variations in the marks even if Jenkinson had taken the same size of shoe, like the tread pattern or width. But the prints were all identical, and therefore they had all been made by one person - John Parsons alias James Jenkinson. I'm sorry, Mr. Jenkinson.'

The Case Of The Ostrich Slasher

'The police will get some bad press if we don't get to the bottom of this one in double quick time, Odell.' Detective Chief Inspector Richmond's expression was one of concern.

Guy N. Smith

The Case of the Ostrich Slasher

'The police will get some bad press if we don't get to the bottom of this one in double quick time, Odell,' Detective Chief Inspector Richmond's expression was one of concern. 'Animal lovers will raise a big stink over a mutilated ostrich than ever they would over a murder. And with this "Phantom Horse slasher", as the press have dubbed him, still at large the public will accuse us of dragging our heels because we are not concerned about animals. Clearly this is the work of a maniac even if it isn't the guy who has already carved up half a dozen horses and ponies.'

'Perhaps.' Raymond Odell was on his hands and knees beside the dead ostrich which resembled a heap of bloodied feathers. His fingers eased back the feathers and revealed several gaping wounds where a sharp blade had delved deep and gouged. 'I would've thought an ostrich would have been a darned sight more difficult to catch and mutilate than an equine, one kick from these birds can kill a man stone dead, and a peck from this beak could... hmmm, that's interesting.' His long slender fingers probed the neck, revealed an abrasion of the skin beneath.

'What is it, Chief?' Tommy Bourne peered over Odell's shoulder.

'Almost as if whoever did this throttled it first,' Odell reached his powerful lens out his pocket, examined the mark intently. Then he held up a strand of what appeared to be coarse hair.

'Any ideas, Odell?' Richmond was anxious; impatient.

'Maybe, maybe not.' Raymond Odell straightened up, smiled. The other two knew well enough that if the detective had found a clue then

THE CASE OF THE OSTRICH SLASHER

he would not reveal it until his deductions were complete. 'I think we'll go and have a chat with the Masons first and see where we go from there.'

'A few years ago ostrich farming was something that was going to make anybody brave enough to change from conventional farming filthy rich,' Don Mason was in his early forties but his features were etched with lines caused by worry. 'Then, as you've probably read in the papers, everything began to fall apart. We're struggling to survive, and the loss of this stud bird will virtually knock us for six. If we could have reared some healthy stock from him then we might've made it. He cost us two grand, now look what some maniac's done to him...and us!'

'Where does one buy birds like ostriches from?' Odell asked as if it was a matter of casual interest.

'A company calling itself Ostrich International Ltd,' Jane, Mason's petite blonde wife, answered. 'A fly-by-night enterprise. They must have taken hundreds of thousands of pounds from folks like ourselves.'

'Do you employ any farm workers?'

'Only at very busy times,' Mason replied. 'Casual labour, if and when we can get it. We were lucky last week, there's a circus comes to town once a year and they camp on a stretch of common about a mile from here. One of the performers needed some extra cash for a few days in between acts. He was a good worker, a guy named Porson. Kept himself to himself, I'd rather it was like that. Don't even know what he did at the circus, I never asked and he didn't volunteer any information. He stopped on for a couple of days after the circus moved on, then left to join them. Don't expect we'll see him again. I can't afford him now,' he added wryly.

'Where's the circus moved to now?' Odell's eyes narrowed.

'They always go from here to Radwick, about twenty miles away. I presume they've followed their regular itinerary this year.'

'Interesting,' Odell said once they were back in the car. 'How do you two fancy a visit to the circus? We better have a word with this Porson fellow but first I think we'll watch a performance incognito. I haven't been since I was a boy.' He laughed softly to himself as Richmond and Tommy exchanged glances.

Jeffrey's Circus was clearly a low budget show as Richmond remarked to Odell as they sat in the sparse audience. The two clowns had been clumsy and unfunny, the trapeze artist's "stunts" were little more than gymnastics. 'And that lion,' Richmond grunted, 'is old and toothless.'

'And sedated,' Odell grimaced.

The lion ambled out of the ring behind Marcus, the trainer. There was a lengthy pause and then Joseph Jeffrey, clad in worn and frayed ringmaster's attire, announced that, 'You are now about to witness, ladies and gentlemen, the cowboy right from the wild west. Allow me to introduce you to Buckaroo Bill!'

Tommy's boredom soon vanished. The cowboy, in authentic clothing, sat on his horse with ease and skill, whirled a lariat with true expertise. Then, from the entrance tunnel, bounded a half-grown calf. Buckaroo Bill whirled his lasso, threw it deftly over the animal's head, rolled it kicking and twisting in a cloud of sawdust. In one perfectly coordinated movement he leapt from his mount, trussed the calf with a length of rope. Then he turned to the audience, swept his Stetson from his head and bowed to the applause.

'I think we'll have a word with Mister Jaffrey after the show,' Odell muttered to Richmond.

'Can't see how all this figures in the business of the mutilated ostrich,' Richmond answered and then fell silent. Whatever his unofficial colleague suspected, he was unlikely to explain until his suspicions were either proved or disproved.

'We're finishing at the end of the summer,' Joseph Jeffrey was clearly ill-at-ease with the presence of the detectives. His caravan was shabby and basic, proof enough that circuses were no longer money-spinning enterprises. 'Kids today don't want circuses, they'd sooner watch videos or play computer games. If we get out this year we'll just about break-even. I was a fool to think that we could make a success of a continental tour. Holland was a disaster, hardly anybody turned up for the shows and we had to hire animals. Marcus refused to perform with a lion he didn't know and we forked out a grand for a blooming ostrich for Buckaroo Bill to lasso. That was the best part of the show.'

'An ostrich?' Odell snapped, 'But you haven't got it now?'

'No,' Jaffrey gave a wry smile. 'Had to go into quarantine. Six bloomin' months without our best act, couldn't afford to wait. So I sold it to a firm I read about in the papers which sells ostriches to farmers. At least I recouped some of my losses that way. They collected it from the quarantine place themselves.'

'I see,' the detective mused. 'Can you remember the name of the firm you sold it to?'

'Some silly name,' Jeffrey tilted his top hat, scratched his thinking grey hair. 'Somethin' like …

yes, I remember now, Ostrich International.'

'Incidentally,' Raymomd Odell's eyes narrowed, 'that lion in the ring tonight. It was sedated.'

'Sure,' Jeffrey dropped his gaze. 'Begbie sees to that, he used to be a vet.'

'Used to be? I thought it was "once a vet, always a vet" even if you weren't actually practicing.'

'He was struck off, some illegal operations he carried out. Served time for it. But he's useful here, keeps the old animals going and mucks in generally.'

'Hmmm.' Odell mused. 'That cowboy, Buckaroo Bill, he seems to know his stuff, alright.'

'He's genuine. Not a cowboy, of course, but he used to be a horse trainer. Begbie found him for us and he's proved to be the best act in the circus. Bill Porson is his real name. If only we could have got the ostrich back here, things might have been different. Mind you,' he added ',over in Amsterdam, we had to give the ostrich a shot of something to quieten it down, otherwise it would have kicked both Bill and his horse out of the ring, maybe gone berserk on the audience, too.'

'Thank you, Mr Jeffrey,' Odell smiled, 'you have been most helpful. Now, my colleagues and I will leave you in peace for an hour or two, although we may have need to return. Might I request that you keep our visit confidential?'

'Oh, sure,' the circus owner looked relieved. 'Last thing I want is for my lot to know the cops have been around making enquiries. You know,' he winked, 'in this game you take on any casuals who come your way and some of them might've done things which are no concern of mine. But so long as they do the work who am I to question their private lives?'

As they walked back across the tract of waste ground upon which the circus was situated, Raymond Odell suddenly stopped and turned. The others watched as he went over to where the horse which Porson had ridden in his act was tethered. Beside it, draped over the fence, was the lasso. Odell lifted up the length of frayed rope, examined it carefully before plucking a strand from it. He placed it carefully in his wallet and Tommy recognised only too well that hint of a smile on his chief's face.

'Any clues?' Richmond voiced his and Tommy's curiosity upon their return to the local police station although he knew only too well that he was wasting his breath.

'We're slowly making progress,' Odell replied non-committal. 'Now, if I may have the use of the station telephone for ten minutes or so I think we might progress even further.'

THE CASE OF THE OSTRICH SLASHER

It was a quarter of an hour before Raymond Odell emerged from the police inspector's private office.

'Richmond,' he addressed his Scotland Yard colleague, 'did you notice, some months ago, an account in the papers about a rather daring robbery in Amsterdam?'

'You mean the theft of the Tiggelovend tiara?' Richmond grunted. 'Interpol circulated us with the details. It was on show at the jewellers and the shop was ram-raided. The thief escaped with the tiara but there was no way such an item would be able to be offered for sale, it is too well known.'

'That's the one.' Raymomd Odell smiled. 'It has never been recovered to this day and the Dutch police don't anticipate ever finding it. Right now it's probably sitting in some crooks private collection.'

'How does that figure in our enquiries?'

'Because that ostrich came from Holland,' Odell replied. 'And then it died in quarantine, I am informed.'

'The customs officers would have noticed if the bird had been wearing the tiara! Anyway, the ostrich is dead.'

'Exactly,' Odell answered. 'The ostrich died but a similar stud bird was purchased from Ostrich International Limited by the Masons.'

Richmond shook his head this was all becoming too involved and unlikely for him, but he knew Odell of old. The private detective had somehow made a connection between the bird that had died and the one that had been savagely mutilated.

'We're going back to Jeffrey's Circus,' Raymond Odell announced. 'The inspector has kindly agreed to co-operate and has delegated a couple of CID officers to accompany us. Unless I miss my guess we are dealing with desperate men.'

This time Raymond Odell did not head directly for Jeffrey's caravan. Instead, followed by Tommy and Richmond with the CID officers bringing up the rear, he walked towards a small crudely constructed corral in which the man who dubbed himself Buckaroo Bill had just lassoed and thrown a lively calf. A second man was kneeling over the trussed animal, a hypodermic syringe in his hand. Both whirled around guiltily at the sound of footfalls.

'What's going on?' The man attempted to conceal the syringe behind his back.

'I might ask you the same question,' Odell pushed open a makeshift gate and stepped inside the enclosure. 'I take it you must be John Begbie?'

'That's me,' the other scowled. 'So what?'

'Just that at the very least my official colleagues

here may arrest you for being in possession of and administering controlled substances. I see that not only do you sedate the poor old lion but you also slow down a lively calf.'

'It's in the interest of public safety,' Begbie backed away a step.

'Perhaps.' Out of the corner of his eye Odell noticed that the other four were now inside the corral. 'I believe both of you went on tour in Holland with the circus last July?'

'That's right,' Porson looks less convincing without his western clothing. 'It wasn't a success.'

'Neither for Mister Jeffrey nor for yourselves,' Raymond Odell's searching gaze flicked from one to the other. 'In fact, many thousand pounds worth of stolen property has gone missing and, it seems, will never come to light again. I refer, of course, to the famous Tiggelovend tiara.'

'Never heard of it,' Begbie growled, took a step backwards.

'Most certainly you have,' Odell saw the two CID men, with Richmond and Tommy, closing in on the vet and the self-styled cowboy. 'In fact, you ram-raided it from an Amsterdam jewellers.'

'That's rubbish,' Porson's laugh was forced.

'No,' Raymond Odell continued, 'you stole the tiara and that's when your problems began. You knew there was no chance of selling such a famous item intact so your prised the valuable diamonds out of it, and the crown itself is probably now residing at the bottom of a fjord. Your other problem was how to smuggle the stones back to England so you hit upon an ingenious plan. Using your veterinary skills, Begbie, you implanted the diamonds in the body of the ostrich which Jeffrey had purchased while on tour. You knew full well that the bird would have to be kept in quarantine upon your return to England but you were prepared to stick with the circus and bide your time until the ostrich was returned to Jeffrey.'

'What a load of rubbish!' Porson laughed again.

'Unfortunately for yourselves,' Odell went on, 'Jeffrey was desperately short of money. So he sold the ostrich straight from quarantine to Ostrich International Ltd who supply breeding stock to ostrich farmers. Unfortunately, the poor bird which carried a fortune around with it died. The Masons, whom you know, purchased an almost identical bird. You contacted Ostrich International, on the pretext of wanting to purchase a fine male bird for stud purposes, and discovered that such a bird had been sold to the Masons. Naturally the firm did not tell you that the bird from quarantine had died. So you had to get the diamonds out of the Mason's bird.'

Porson and Begbie glanced around them

THE CASE OF THE OSTRICH SLASHER

uneasily; the three policemen and Tommy had moved in on them.

'Porson, you took a casual job at the Masons' farm to suss out the situation, and you were convinced that the stud ostrich there was the same one that you and Begbie had put the diamonds inside. By this time the feathers would have grown again over the incisions where the diamonds were implanted and you wouldn't know for certain if it was the one until you started cutting it open. Catching an ostrich is far from easy.' Raymond Odell smiled. 'So the other evening you went to the Masons' farm after dark and Buckaroo Bill performed this act for real and lassoed the ostrich. For your information, a strand from the frayed lariat,' Odell pointed to the rope that dangled from Porson's grasp, 'adhered to the feathers and I have since matched it with the rope it came from, the one you are now holding. I was also puzzled by the wounds in the ostrich; a maniac would have slashed and stabbed, but these were deep gouges and probes. I concluded that the attacker was hacking for something specific beneath the skin rather than simply inflicting a series of cruel wounds. My conversations with Ostrich International and Interpol completed my jigsaw and now …'

Begbie and Porson sprang into action, would

have dashed for the fence and tried to escape, but the detectives were too quick for them. Tommy's rugby tackle brought down Porson, whilst the CID officers leaped upon Begbie and bore him to the ground.

From the doorway of his battered caravan, Jeffrey watched and shook his head sadly. His touring circus would not even last until the end of the year now.

'Well, I never thought a senseless act like the slashing of an ostrich would lead to the solving of an international crime,' Richmond shook his head in disbelief.

'Which just goes to show,' Raymond Odell laughed, 'that you never know what the outcome will be when you embark upon the most seemingly trivial of investigations. I treat them all the same initially, no detail must be overlooked, no matter how irrelevant it might seem. As they say, you never know…'

The Bomb

The collar-bar of the 'Highwayman' was packed to capacity when the bomb went off. Tom Llewellyn, the Licencee, was in the process of pulling a pint when the deafening explosion reduced the small city tavern to a shambles in a matter of seconds.

Guy N. Smith

The Bomb

The cellar-bar of the 'Highwayman' was packed to capacity when the bomb went off. Tom Llewellyn, the licencee, was in the process of pulling a pint when the deafening explosion reduced the small city tavern to a shambles in a matter of seconds. The lights went out, the ceiling came down, and then the screaming began. It was 10.20 p.m. when the first ambulance arrived on the scene of the disaster.

'I'm obliged to you for turning out, Odell,' Detective-Inspector Richmond grimaced as he and Raymond Odell, the famous detective, stepped amidst the ruins of the 'Highwayman'. Everywhere C.I.D. men worked feverishly. The atmosphere was thick with dust, and Tommy Bourne, Odell's young assistant, coughed involuntarily.

'A nasty business,' Raymond Odell remarked, his keen eyes missing nothing.

'Fortunately,' the Yard man replied, 'there's only one fatality – Llewellyn, the licencee. Six injured, though. It could have been a lot worse. There's too much of this lately. I never thought I'd see the day when terrorism was rife in England!'

The detective said nothing. Instead, he was on his hands and knees examining something carefully with the aid of his powerful lens.

'What is it?' Richmond was always hopeful when anything interested his unofficial colleague. He had great faith in the other's seemingly superhuman powers.

Odell was extracting an envelope from his wallet, and into it he scooped what looked like particle of powdered brick-dust.

'What's so unusual about that?' Richmond was disappointed as he saw his companion's find. 'You could collect that by the bucketful in here. Most of the masonry from the inside wall crumbled with the blast!'

'This isn't masonry,' Raymond Odell's eyes were gleaming. 'And furthermore, it's foreign to any building components used in this place. Now, let me see, where was the bomb hidden?'

'Just here,' Richmond replied, 'in this corner where there was a juke-box until it was disintegrated by the explosion.'

'Adjoining the bar,' Odell was definitely puzzled. 'So, in effect, although the device used was a comparatively small one, the person who planted it could only be certain of killing the licencee who would be serving right by it, and any unfortunate customer who happened to be using the juke-box at the time it went off. As it happened, nobody was, so it was just poor Mr. Llewellyn who got blown to smithereens!'

'We'll be making a series of dawn swoops on known terrorists,' Detective-Inspector Richmond had the utmost confidence in his men. 'There's a good chance we'll pick him up then.'

'Personally, I wouldn't think so,' Raymond Odell led the way out into the refreshing night air in the street above. It was dry and frosty. He stood for a moment, stuffing tobacco into his blackened briar pipe, a thoughtful look on his face. 'We shan't be able to do much before tomorrow, Richmond.

However, tomorrow morning there are two things which I want done. Firstly, I want Tommy to take the contents of this envelope round to the British Museum. I have no doubt that they will be able to tell us where this type of stone comes from. Secondly, if it could be arranged, I'd like to interview Tom Llewellyn's widow. Until then, I don't think there's much more that we can do.'

Raymond Odell wished that he did not have to question Gladys Llewellyn. Her doctor had given her some mild sedation, and at times she appeared to be unaware of what was going on. All the same, the detective knew that he had to persevere with this interrogation. It meant the difference between a murderer being brought to trial or going free!

'How long is it since you first came to the 'Highwayman', Mrs. Llewellyn?' his tones were patient and kindly.

'Less than a year,' she sobbed. 'Oh, if only we had stopped at the 'Grasshopper' at Llanadevy, this terrible thing would never have happened. He would not have moved except for the fact that Tom's brother, Gwynne, came back to live in the village after their father died. The old man was a hill-farmer in a small way, but his 90-acre farm was left to the two boys. Tom and Gwynne got on so well, too, but Tom just wasn't interested in going on the farm, so he let his brother carry on with it. He still had a share in it, of course, a sleeping partner you might call it. Then the quarry people wanted to buy the farm for quarrying. Tom hadn't the guts to say 'no', although it hurt him to think of his old family home being quarried up. He could've put a stop to it, but Tom wasn't that sorry. We'd got the pub in the village at the time, and Gwynne was still negotiating with the quarrying people, haggling over a price, always trying to get them to agree to a bigger one. Then, I suppose he would have come along, and persuaded Tom to sign away his half of the farm as well. I think Tom would have done, now that we'd been away from Llanadevy for a bit. Pity it didn't happen sooner. We'd've been able to retire then, and we wouldn't have been… here… for this!'

'When did you last see Gwynne Llewellyn?' Odell asked.

'Oh, not since we left Llanadevy,' the other replied. 'The city was another world to him. He'd never been out of the Welsh Hills in his life. Before he came to the farm. He'd worked in a quarry for ten years. I suppose that was where he'd got the idea of selling out to the quarry people. Got some knowledge of the type of land they were after, I suppose.'

Odell and Richmond left the small city flat where the Llewellyns had lived for the past ten months, made their way back across Piccadilly, and into Dover Street. Odell's housekeeper opened the door of her room as she heard them coming up the stairs.

'Oh, Mr. Odell,' she said, 'a message from Mr. Bourne. He's been kept waiting at the British Museum, but he should be back in an hour or so.'

Raymond Odell ushered Richmond into his consulting room, and, taking off their hats and coats, the former poured out two glasses of sherry.

'Here's to our success, Richmond,' he smiled as they touched glasses. 'So far the pieces of this jigsaw are scattered, but I'm hoping it won't be too long before we're able to fit some of them together.'

'My men have pulled in a dozen known terrorists,' Richmond smiled, and sipped his drink. 'If any one of them planted that bomb, my chaps will get it out of him. If not, then at least we'll have the pleasure of getting the Home Secretary to sign a few expulsion orders. All the same, I can't see how the lines which *you're* pursuing will help.'

Odell smiled, and his colleague had learned, long ago, that all would be revealed in due course, and, until then, further questions would be futile.

THE BOMB

*   *   *

'Well, Tommy,' Odell's expression reminded his young assistant of a bloodhound waiting to be unleashed on the trail of some hunted man, 'what did the British Museum make of my little find?'

'They said it's slate dust,' the young detective replied. 'Once you get it on yourself you're likely to carry it around with you until you have a change of clothes. It gets on the soles of your shoes and will stop there for days during dry weather. This type is found mostly in Wales.'

Raymond Odell brough his fist down on the table with a resounding thump.

'That's it!' His eyes had that gleam which both of them knew only too well. 'There us a light in the darkness at last, Richmond, but we still have much work to do. Tommy and I are leaving for Wales first thing in the morning. Can you come with us?'

'The terrorists we're questioning…' the Yard man began, but Odell cut him short.

'Come with me, Richmond,' he said, 'and I'll guarantee that you have your cowardly bomber under lock and key before the end of the week!'

'Goodness me, Odell!' Detective-Inspector Richmond paused, breathing heavily, and looking down the slope which they had just scaled. 'Surely there's an easier route to Llanadevy Farm than this? There must be a track whereby we could have taken the car right up to the farmhouse!'

Odell smiled, the last afternoon sun shining on his aquiline face.

'I want to have a look round first before we go and introduce ourselves to Mr. Gwynne Llewellyn.' He suddenly stopped and pointed to a small crater on the hillside above them. 'They could be just what we're looking for!'

Tommy and Richmond scrambled in the wake of the detective whose energy seemed endless. Even after having driven a full two hundred miles from London, he was still as fresh as when he had started out.

Raymond Odell paused on the brink of that rocky crater which he had spotted from further down. It was about twenty yards in circumference, its depth varying from three to ten feet. All around was a mass of crumbled stone, forming a jagged and untidy mess.

'This reminds me of one of those 25-pounders the Jerries used to drop in the war,' Richmond puffed as he and Tommy joined Odell.

The detective stooped down, and picked up a handful of rubble, sorting out some of the split and crushed stone which he exhibited in the palm of his hand.

THE BOMB

'What's that remind you of?' he asked them, a gleam of excitement in his steely eyes.

'Why... why... it's identical to that substance, you found amongst the rubble at the 'Highwayman',' Richmond gasped.

'Right first time!' Odell snapped. 'It's *slate*! This hillside is mostly slate beneath the scrub and heather. Furthermore, this hole has been recently blasted out. I think we've seen all we need. Come on!'

Stumbling and sliding, Richmond and Tommy followed in the wake of the famous detective who seemed to be as fleet-footed as a mountain goat. Tommy could not help regretting that they had not brought Ben, their bloodhound, along with them for some much needed exercise in these Welsh mountains.

Dusk was just falling as they saw the small white-washed farmhouse nestling in the hollow beneath them. Around it, the outbuildings had a distinct appearance of neglect. It had the atmosphere of a farm which had been discarded by its owner. A light was showing in one of the windows.

As they approached the house, they could see the occupant through the window, sitting in front of a log fire. He was shabbily dressed, with a shock of white hair flopping over his forehead. There was three-day growth of stubble on his chin, and his eyes flitted nervously around the room. He leapt from his chair as Raymond Odell pounded on the door.

'Mr. Llewellyn?' the detective asked as the door was opened a foot or so, and the gaunt face peered at them from within.

'Yes,' the other snapped, all the time narrowing the gap by pushing the door shut an inch at a time. Only Odell's foot prevented it being slammed in their faces.

'We want to talk to you, Mr. Llewellyn,' Odell's voice was terse. 'My name's Raymond Odell. This is Detective-Inspector Richmond of Scotland Yard!'

'My God!' the other's face was suddenly pallid beneath its natural tan. He released his hold on the door, and, pushing it open, Odell entered, followed by the other two.

'What d'you want? Can't a man be left in peace in his own house?' he whined, his sing-song accent depicting sheer terror.

'We want to ask you about an explosion in a public-house in London, known as the 'Highwayman',' Raymond Odell stood with his back to the living room door, Tommy Bourne and Richmond on either side of him. 'It is fondly

THE BOMB

supposed to have been perpetrated by terrorists. We think otherwise!'

'I... I...' Llewellyn looked about him, seeking any possible avenue of escape, but there was none. He stammered something unintelligible, and then flopped back into his chair.

'Let me tell you what I know,' the detective leaned against the mantleshelf, filling his pipe. Yet his vigilance was not relaxed. His eyes never left the frightened man. 'Your father's will stated that this farm was to go to yourself and your brother,' he went on, 'but you did not fancy the idea of farm work for the rest of your life. You knew that these quarrying companies paid high prices for land such as this which is a veritable bed of slate. You had been a quarry man yourself. You knew the procedure. You had contacts. No doubt that was how you obtained the gelignite and the timing mechanism with which to make your bomb!'

The other sank his head in his hands, trembling, but Raymond Odell continued with scarcely a paise.

'You saw a way to kill your brother, obtain his share of the proceeds when you sold the farm for quarrying, and retire to a life of luxury. Of course, not being conversant with the law, you would not realise that his half would have gone to his wife... or perhaps you were hoping that she would be helping behind the bar so that you could eliminate them both! A check will no doubt show that you travelled to Shrewsbury with your home-made bomb, took a train to London, and, choosing a crowded evening when your brother's pub would be full, and there was little likelihood of him seeing you, you stole in, planted your device as near to the bar as you could, and took the next train back home. You probably put on your best suit, but you travelled in your ordinary everyday shoes! I can see from here that the soles are plastered with slate dust. I see also that you have permitted the quarry firm to carry out some experimental blasting to ascertain the depth of the slate on your land. The weather being dry, you carried the slate dust as far as your brother's pub. Only tiny particles were left amidst the debris of your destruction, but it was sufficient to catch my eye amongst the red brick-dust!'

Gwynne Llewellyn was sobbing quietly to himself as Richmond stepped forward, and placed a heavy hand on his shoulder.

'You thought the terrorists, who are at present carrying out a wave of this type of bombing, would be blamed, didn't you?' he grunted. 'Well, we're not quite as easy to fool as that at Scotland Yard, you know!'

THE BOMB

Raymond Odell and Tommy Bourne smiled at each other.

Guy N. Smith

The Perfect Murder

'I'd be glad of your help in this matter, Odell.' Detective-Inspector Richmond of Scotland Yard looked across his desk at Raymond Odell, the famous detective, and Tommy Bourne.

Guy N. Smith

The Perfect Murder

'I'd be glad of your help in this matter, Odell,' Detective-Inspector Richmond of Scotland Yard looked across his desk at Raymond Odell, the famous detective, and Tommy Bourne, the latter's young assistant. 'This is as near the perfect murder as we're ever likely to come across. In fact, I really don't see much chance of us proving Gidman's guilt.'

'Well, if you'd like to fill us in on the details,' Odell was filling his blackened briar pipe as he spoke, 'then Tommy and I will be only too pleased to come down to Lincolnshire with you and have a look round Gidman's place, and his private airfield.'

'Ronald Gidman is a wealthy man with a thriving export business,' Richmond began. 'In fact, for the last two or three years he has been leaving the running of his business to Rich Corda, his manager and general factotum, whilst he pursued his life-long hobby of flying. He owns a small plane which he keeps in a hangar on a piece of ground adjoining this country home of his, close to the shores of the Nash. However, Corda had been carrying on with Sheila Gidman for some time behind Ronald's back. Ronald found out and threatened to kill him. However, a couple of nights ago the Gidmans invited Corda round to their place. A sort of 'make-up-and-let's-be-friends' gathering. The three of them drank until after midnight. Shelia Gidman was the first one to retire to bed. According to her, Ronald came up about an hour later. He swears that Corda went up to his room at the same time. He might have done, but the bed was never slept in. In fact, there was no sign of Corda at all next morning. He never even showed up at the business premises in Spalding. Then, late yesterday afternoon, a trawler picked up his body several miles out in the North Sea. There was a gash in the back of his head as though he had been struck down from behind with some blunt instrument. Yet, the strangest factor of all was the charred remains of a parachute harness which was attached to his body!'

'You mean he had parachuted down in the sea?' Odell asked. 'Presumably he took the plane out, and it caught fire.'

Richmond shook his head.

'Nothing of the kind,' he said. 'You see, Gidman's plane was the only one for miles around. Apart from everything else, Corda hadn't a clue how to fly a plane. Even if he had been a first class pilot, he couldn't have got the plane off the ground. The engine was all in bits. Gidman is one of these fanatics who derives more pleasure from taking his machine to bits than flying it! Our experts have examined the small runway. No aircraft has been on it for weeks!'

'I see!' Odell blew clouds of tobacco smoke up towards the ceiling, and his brows knitted together. 'So we have a body floating out at sea which has come from the one place in the area where there is an aircraft, and that aircraft is incapable of becoming airborne! A motive, but absolutely no proof. I think, Richmond, that we had better come down to Lincolnshire with you. Tommy can nip back and put one or two things in an overnight case for us. Then we can be on our way.'

Ronald Gidman was a suave handsome man in his early forties. His wife, Shelia, was blonde-haired, some ten years younger than himself, and very attractive. They gave no sign that recently their marriage had been on the verge of breaking-up.

'A terrible business, gentleman,' Gidman said as he escorted Richmond, Odell, and Tommy round the grounds. 'Richard Corda was a very good friend of ours in spite of a recent storm in a teacup. How his body came to be floating out at sea I haven't the faintest idea. As far as Shelia and I were concerned, he was fast asleep in bed, in the room which he always used when he stayed here.'

'Do you keep any parachutes?' Odell asked casually.

'There are a couple in the plane,' Gidman replied. 'They've never been unwrapped since I bought them. Anyway, come on into the hangar, and I'll show you the set-up.'

The hangar was an ex-wartime corrugated-iron structure, just large enough to house the small single-engined aircraft. Odell casually glanced at the neatly wrapped parachutes. Obviously they had never been opened. Piece of the engine were laid out on a wooden bench just inside the door. There was no question, whatsoever, that the aeroplane would require another couple of days' work before it was capable of flying.

Raymond Odell noticed some large cylinders lying in the corner of the hangar. He was surprised that he was able to lift one without any trouble at all. The outer casing was rusted, and it was obviously empty.

'These are old helium cylinders aren't they?' he murmured, dropping it on to the floor.

'That's right,' Gidman smiled. 'I bought this hangar as a job-lot. All the junk that had lain in it since the war was delivered with it. I've been meaning to get the local scrap-merchant to call round and take most of it away.'

They went back outside. The grassy runway ran parallel to the garden, heading towards the saltmarshes. In the distance they could see the mudflats shimmering in the sunlight. The tide was fully two miles out.

Raymond Odell looked thoughtful as they trudged back to the house for lunch. Whilst Richmond was engaged in conversation with Gidman, he drew Tommy Bourne to one side.

'I want you to do something for me, Tommy,' he whispered. 'As inconspicuously as possible. Just down the road there is a telephone kiosk. I want you to telephone the meteorological-office and ascertain the force and direction of the wind in this area at midnight on the night before last.'

Tommy looked puzzled, but he knew better than to question his chief. Raymond Odell never did anything without a reason, and he would not explain anything until he was ready. The young detective lagged behind the others, and then, when nobody seemed to be paying any attention to him, he set on his mission.

It was not until after lunch that Tommy had a chance to speak to Odell alone.

'I got the information you wanted, chief,' he whispered. 'The winds were westerly and freshening.'

'Ah!' There was a gleam in the other's eyes which told Tommy that that was what Odell had hoped to hear. 'Most interesting, Tommy. Now, it seems that the Gidmans are fully occupied with Richmond so I suggest that we go and have another look in the hangar whilst the coast is clear.'

Ten minutes later the two detectives were rummaging through the piles of junk at the far end of the hangar.

THE PERFECT MURDER

'What are we looking for, chief?' Tommy asked as he tossed aside coils of rusty wire and empty cartons.

'Speaking purely from memories of the wartime days,' Raymond Odell paused to light his pipe again, 'the object I want to find is about the size and shape of a matchbox with a little dial on top. Of course, it's only a hunch. There may be none here.'

Five minutes later it was Tommy who gave a gasp of triumph and held aloft an object such as his chief had described.

'Well done, Tommy!' Odell snatched it from him. 'So I was right after all!'

'Whatever is it?' Tommy asked.

'It's a…' but Odell never finished his sentence, for at that moment the door opened, and Richmond and Gidman entered.

'Ah, there you are, Odell,' the Yard man boomed. 'We've been looking all over the place for you. Whatever are you doing amongst all that rubbish?'

'Poking his nose in, and taking liberties,' Gidman snarled, every trace of his former composure having disappeared.

'Then perhaps you would be good enough to explain this away,' Raymond Odell held the small object aloft for Gidman to see. 'Also these empty helium cannisters.'

'I told you earlier,' the other replied. 'It was all junk that came from the airfield with the hangar.'

'I've no doubt it did,' the detective replied. 'But everything else is covered in dirt and dust, whilst these have been handled recently. There's a whole box of these incendiary timing-devices, and the seal has been broken recently!'

Fear replaced anger on Gidman's face. He hesitated, and then made a sudden dive for the open door. It was Richmond's outstretched foot which brought him down, and Tommy Bourne was on him at once. Between them they hauled him to his feet.

'Alright, alright,' Gidman wheezed, 'take it easy. You've got nothing on me!'

'I wouldn't be too sure of that,' replied Raymond Odell. 'I know now how you killed Richard Corda, and transported his body out into the North Sea.'

'Oh, yeah!' Gidman jeered. 'Then go ahead. Let's hear it, Mr. Odell. I can't wait for a good laugh!'

'Well,' began Raymond Odell. 'After your spot of bother, when you discovered that Corda was having an affair with your wife, things seemed peaceful enough. But Richard Corda wasn't giving up so easily. Neither was your wife. You found out that it was still going on, so you decided that the only sure way to stop it was to kill Corda. It presented problems, though. Obviously, you would be number one suspect. Then, suddenly, you hit upon an idea for something for which every killer has been searching for centuries – *the perfect murder*! It all came to you, no doubt, when you were foraging amongst the junk in here. You found some small barrage-balloons, cylinders of helium, and incendiary-timing devices.

'After your wife had retired to bed, you managed to persuade Corda to come out to the hangar with you on some pretext. Then you struck him down from behind. I doubt whether we shall ever discover the weapon. It is probably at the bottom of the sea by now. Anyway, you had prepared everything beforehand, and it did not take many minutes to fasten the body to the balloon with an old parachute harness. You fixed one of these devices on to the straps, probably timing it to go off in a couple of hours or so. Then, you inflated the balloon with helium gas. No doubt you had checked wind force and direction earlier. I checked this afternoon. At the time of the murder there was a freshening westerly wind which would take your contraption out across the Wash to the North Sea.'

'Go on,' all three of them knew by Gidman's expression that Odell's theory was correct. Yet, the exporter was determined to bluff until the very end. 'You really ought to take up writing detective stories, Mr. Odell.'

Raymond Odell ignored the remark and continued with his story. 'Obviously, everything went to plan. After a couple of hours or so the incendiary went off and deposited the body and the murder-weapon in the sea, destroying the balloon at the same time. If the corpse was never found, Corda would just be listed as missing. If it was located, then the police would be looking for a mysterious aeroplane, and a pilot who had murdered Corda for some obscure reason. You made sure that your own aircraft was well out of action so that no suspicion could fall upon yourself.'

Ronald Gidman was silent.

'Very nearly the perfect murder,' Raymond Odell concluded. 'Oh, so very nearly. But you had to go and spoil it all through carelessness and laziness. If you had just taken the trouble to dispose of these empty cylinders and remaining incendiary devices, there would have been no evidence to link you with the killing!'

'Well, we could have saved ourselves the trouble of packing our overnight cases,' Odell remarked as the three of them set out on the long drive back to London.

'Quite frankly, I didn't expect to be seeing the Yard again for another fortnight,' Richmond did not hide his praises for his unofficial colleague.

'A bit of luck, combined with a few mistakes on the part of the murderer,' Raymond Odell replied, 'and we had him. I'm always sceptical about these so-called 'perfect' murders. No murder is perfect. There's always a flaw somewhere. It's just a case of spotting it!'

Guy N. Smith

The Poisoners

'I'm going out to walk the dogs'. Frances Agnew, Fran to most of her friends, called up the stairs to where her husband Shane was tapping away on his computer.

'Okay.' there was a pause. ' No need to lock the door. I won't be going anywhere.'

Guy N. Smith

The Poisoners

'I'm going out to walk the dogs', Frances Agnew, Fran to most of her friends, called up the stairs to where her husband Shane was tapping away on his computer.

'Okay,' there was a pause. 'No need to lock the door, I won't be going anywhere.'

'See you later then.' Both dogs were tugging at their leads in anticipation of their daily walk. They were border collies, Enzo, a red and white dog,

Casey a black and white bitch. Eager to get into Fiddle Woods that adjoined Mill Bank village, a quiet and rural community about a mile from Ripponden and Sowerby Bridge.

Once clear of the village Fran let the dogs loose, setting them bounding to and fro. It was a lovely sunny morning in late spring.

Back home Shane was studying some information which had just come through on his computer. He worked from home for a commercial software company and in recent weeks he had been engaged on a project named VINE. Currently he was perfecting a complex algorithm.

Amidst his deep concentration he heard a click of the front door as it opened. Surely Fran wasn't back already!

Footsteps on the stairs. The door of the small room which he used as an office creaked.

'Everything okay?' He did not turn his head. 'You can't have had a very long walk…'

Suddenly there was a man in the room, slightly built, a cap pulled down over his forehead and a dark cloth tied over his face.

'What the… who the hell are you?'

Just an answering grunt and then the stranger was upon him, a strong arm encircling his neck, pulling him backwards, seconds later Shane was sprawled in a motionless heap on the floor, his attacker stooping over him.

'I'm back,' Fran called up from the bottom of the stairs. 'I'll start the lunch…'

There was no reply from upstairs. Both dogs were crouched under the table, shaking.

'Whatever's the matter with you two?' she said to her trembling canines.

A sudden sense of foreboding flooded over her and she ran for the stairs.

'Oh my god!' She stared at the sight of her husband sprawled on the floor. On his desk his computer was smashed, broken parts strewn all around.

She went back downstairs, composed herself and in a faltering tone called the police.

Paramedics and police arrived within a remarkably short time, Inspector Boyd escorted Fran into the living room, did his utmost to pacify her. He explained that he would return in due course and take a statement from her.

In the meantime, Shane's corpse was being carried downstairs to be loaded into the ambulance where it would be taken for examination to determine the cause of death.

There was no sign of the software which the computer contained. 'I assume you didn't know,' the stocky Detective Inspector Boyd told Fran, 'your husband was engaged in some top security work. I cannot give you any details'

'I guessed as much,' the trembling Fran replied. 'He never spoke about his work.'

'Which is doubtless why he was murdered' the other replied. 'Possibly by a foreign agent who had come to this country in one of those exchanges of spies. It will all come out in due course. Hey, those dogs of yours are extremely interested in their deceased master's body. Call them off, please.'

With some difficulty Fran managed to bring the two dogs under control. It was as though they had scented something of interest on Shane's corpse. Boyd bent down to examine where the dogs had been and noticed a small scratch just behind Shane's right ear.

After the police left Fran made a phone call. Raymond Odell, the private detective, had long been a good friend of her husband's. Who better to get to the bottom of this terrible business?

Odell answered the phone in his Midland office. He was clearly shocked by Fran's news.

'I'll be with you later today,' he promised.

'Hmm,' Odell, accompanied by his assistant, Tommy Bourne, Examined the murder room. The police had taken the remnants of the wrecked computer.

Suddenly Fran's visitors were joined by her two dogs, Enzo and Casey. There was no mistaking their enthusiasm as they sniffed around the room.

'They're tracker dogs' Fran explained. Both dogs belonged to the North Canine dog search team.

'In which case,' the detective replied, 'we'll take them out and see if they can pick up a scent, maybe lead us to the murderer if he is still in the vicinity.'

Tommy had both dogs on leashes, it was as much as he could do to hold them as, noses to the ground, they led the way out of the small village into a steep wooded area which led to the old Park Hall, the once grand house of the local mill owner, now a holiday rental.

Suddenly Enzo stopped and indicated with a bark.

'Whatever has he found,' Fran stooped down and picked up a small bag containing phials and hypodermic needles.

'Now what the hell is this about?' The detective muttered. 'It has obviously been dumped, wouldn't have been found were it not for these dogs.' Both dogs were tugging on their leads again. Obviously, the scent they had been following continued further, on to the woodland beyond.

'We'll go back,' Odell announced. 'I want to think this through. If the murderer is still in the vicinity, we have to find him.'

'I've just had a thought,' Fran stated suddenly. 'My own computer's in the bedroom. Nobody has thought of looking at it. Sometimes Shane used it. There could be something there – a clue maybe – to all of this.

'There's an unsent email here,' Odell opened up Fran's computer. 'It appears to be a work colleague at the software company for whom Shane had worked for some time. Strangely the last sentence appeared to be unfinished ending with the words *VINE near completion*.

'It's as though he was concerned about the security of his work and used your computer to send this message, which is unfinished because he got interrupted, maybe by a phone call. Then for some reason he returned to his study where he was murdered. Tomorrow we'll return to where the dogs found the bag and see if they can follow the scent further.'

* * *

THE POISONERS

The following morning Odell, Tommy and Fran were back in the wood where the dogs had last found the scent they were following.

Tommy was straining to hold back the dogs on their leads. Clearly the scent was still strong enough, fortunately it had not rained overnight.

Fighting their way through the undergrowth, they emerged before the entrance of a disused clay mine where in years gone by clay had been excavated for the Knowles Pipe works at the bottom of the valley. Truly an eerie place but the dogs were pulling even harder, whining at their excitement.

Odell's torch lit up the huge cave, its walls dripping with condensation – it was bitterly cold.

'The dogs are going crazy,' Tommy muttered. 'God knows what, or who, we're going to find in here!'

No sooner had he spoken than a figure appeared out of the darkness, a man in tight fitting overalls, a cap pulled down over his forehead. His features were swarthy, muttering threats in a foreign language.

In his raised hand was a crude wooden club, obviously broken from one of the trees outside. He grabbed Fran, presumably to take a hostage but Fran lashed out at the assailant's face, striking him hard enough to cause him to recoil.

Odell knew he had to act fast. In one lightning-quick move, he sprang forward, his clenched fist taking their adversary on the point of his chin with every ounce of strength which the detective could muster.

The man fell back, hit his head on the rocky wall and slumped to the ground, lying huddled and motionless.

'I don't think he'll be going anywhere for a while,' there was no mistaking the relief in Odell's voice. 'Now we'd better call up Inspector Boyd and get the cops up here to take this monstrosity into custody. Maybe then we'll know more about this business.'

It was the following morning when Odell, Tommy and Fran met with Inspector Boyd in the Agnew household.

'I must congratulate you, Odell, on bringing Mr Agnew's murderer to justice. He was a North Korean, part of their Embassy team, believe it or not, apparently on an official visit to discuss trade with our government. We assume they were concerned about Shane's work, so decided to remove him. VINE was a secret Government project enabling communication worldwide to be decrypted enabling us to intercept North Korean secrets and intelligence information. Hence, the man who was perfecting the algorithm had to be removed. Shane had tried to send that email from his wife's computer as a safeguard maybe assuming his computer was compromised. Sadly, he was interrupted and murdered before he could complete it.

'I say *was*, as the killer, Kim Jae Rok, died on the way to the station before we had a chance to question him. It appears that he had been injected with some of the same chemical that killed Shane.'

Fran turned away to hide her expression. Neither Odell nor Tommy had seen Fran slip a hand into that plastic bag found in the woods the previous day and remove one of the syringes. She had surreptitiously slipped it into her jacket pocket and when the assailant had grabbed her in the clay mine he had given her the perfect opportunity to use it. Nobody would ever know that it was her who had delivered the fatal injection in revenge for her husband's murder.

That evening when Odell and everyone had left, and the dogs had settled down next to Fran's feet, the mobile rung – number withheld.

'Hello,' Fran answered.

'Well done Frances on your successful mission. Nice touch silencing the other agent,' came back the reply from the caller speaking in English but with a heavy Korean accent.

Fran hung up and patted Casey's head. 'We will miss him.'

The Case Of The Flying Corpse

Detective-Inspector Richmond of the C.I.D. has called upon his old colleague Raymond Odell, a private detective, to help him with a particularly difficult case.

Guy N. Smith

The Case of the Flying Corpse

Publisher's note:

What follows is a comic strip, originally self-published in Adventure Strip Weekly and drawn by Peter Knifton.

The rest of the story was never published and despite our best searches, no copies of the conclusion have been found.

It is presumed the comic strip was never completed and sadly Guy does not have any notes on how the story was to end.

However, in order to make The Casebook Of Raymond Odell as complete a resource of the character's adventures as possible, we present the opening, and all that exists, of The Case Of The Flying Corpse.

RAYMOND ODELL: THE CASE OF THE FLYING CORPSE...

DETECTIVE-INSPECTOR RICHMOND OF THE C.I.D. HAS CALLED UPON HIS OLD COLLEAGUE RAYMOND ODELL, A PRIVATE DETECTIVE, TO HELP HIM WITH A PARTICULARLY DIFFICULT CASE.

"THIS IS A TOUGH ONE ODELL, THE NEAREST I'VE EVER COME TO THE 'PERFECT MURDER'. RONALD GIDMAN HAS AN EXPORT BUSINESS CLOSE TO THE WASH, HIS HOBBY IS FLYING, AND HE OWNS A SMALL PLANE WHICH HAS BEEN DISMANTLED FOR OVERHAULING FOR THE LAST FEW WEEKS. NOW GIDMAN IS KNOWN TO HAVE A FEUD WITH HIS PERSONAL SECRETARY, RICHARD CORDA. TWO DAYS AGO A BOAT PICKED UP THE CHARRED REMAINS OF CORDA'S BODY AT SEA. THE REMNANTS OF A PARACHUTE HARNESS ON HIM."

"THERE WAS A WOUND IN THE BACK OF THE HEAD AS HE'D BEEN CLUBBED DOWN. HE LIVED IN A FLAT IN THE GIDMAN'S HOUSEHOLD, AND HE'D BEEN TALKING TO THEM ON THE NIGHT HE DISAPPEARED. OBVIOUSLY AN AEROPLANE HAD DROPPED HIM IN THE SEA, YET THE ONLY PLANE WAS GIDMAN'S AND IT WAS IN THE HANGAR."

"I'LL COME DOWN TO LINCOLNSHIRE WITH YOU, RICHMOND."

LATER

"BRINGS BACK MEMORIES OF WARTIME DAYS DOESN'T IT?"

"ALL THAT WAS DELIVERED WITH THE HELIUM WHEN I BOUGHT. IT BEEN MEANING TO GET RID OF IT."

HELIUM GAS

ODELL AND RICHMOND TOOK A STROLL ALONG THE SEAWALL.

"WHAT'S THAT?"

"SOUNDS LIKE A CRY FOR HELP, COME ON!"

HELP!!!

"THAT WAS CLOSE. NOW HEY, WHAT ARE THESE?"

"THEY WERE JUST LYING THERE, HONEST, AND WHEN I TRIED TO GET TO EM I FELL IN THE QUICKSANDS."

Guy N. Smith

FIRST PUBLICATION LISTING

The following details the first known publications of the stories in this collection:

The Making Of A Detective – Caerlaverock # 20 (1975)

The Fatal Smoke – Caerlaverock # 22 (1975)

The Garrotter – Caerlaverock # 24 (1976)

Faithful Betrayal – Caerlaverock # 25 (1976)

The Curse Of The Crystal – Caerlaverock # 27 (1976)

Death On The Stairs – Caerlaverock # 28 (1976)

Dressed To Kill – Thing # 7 & 8 (1972)

Concrete Evidence – Thing # 10 & 11 (1972)

THE CASEBOOK OF RAYMOND ODELL

FIRST PUBLICATION LISTING

Quick-Change Artist – Thing # 12, 13 & 14 (1973)

The Case Of The Ostrich Slasher – Graveyard Rendezvous # 16 (1997)

The Bomb – previously unpublished

The Perfect Murder – previously unpublished

The Poisoners – previously unpublished

The Case Of The Flying Corpse – Adventure Strip Weekly (1976)

Guy N. Smith

ABOUT THE AUTHOR

Guy N. Smith has been a best-selling author for over 40 years. He has written over 70 horror novels since 1975 as well as numerous short stories in the genre. He continues to publish books every year.

Find out more at www.guynsmith.com

THE CASEBOOK OF RAYMOND ODELL

Also from the Sinister Horror Company

The Charnel Caves: A Crabs Novel

Horror lurked in the maze of cliff caves where a new generation of giant crabs were breeding.

In 1975 an army of gigantic crabs, the result of an underwater nuclear experiment, attacked the Welsh coastline.

The battle was bloody, many lives were lost until the crustacean invaders were defeated.

Over the ensuing years they turned up in the oceans of the World with further terrible slaughter of humans. Finally, though, it was believed that these monsters from the deep had been eradicated. Only memories of their invasions of land remained with the older inhabitants, tales of their depredations on mankind were whispered but often ridiculed by the modern generations.

Until a few of the survivors returned to the Welsh coast and began breeding secretly in a maze of caverns beneath the cliffs, preparing for a further attack on mankind.

Guy N. Smith Illustrated Bibliography

"The sheer effort and dedication that's gone into creating this unbelievably comprehensive bibliography is breath-taking." – DLS Reviews

The complete(ish) guide to collecting the works of Guy N. Smith.

A journey into collecting the works of prolific author Guy Newman Smith. The book covers all genres of the Great Scribbler's writing and contains over 950 pictures and useful details to assist any would-be collector.

Guy N. Smith Illustrated Bibliography

The author has endeavoured to list and visually represent, through over 950 colour pictures, the vast catalogue of output from Guy N. Smith's 65+ years in print; from the early stories he had published in the Tettenhall Observer and Advertiser paper as a teenager through to the present day. A career that crosses fiction and non-fiction and has covered almost all possible genres along the way, from Self-Sufficiency to Westerns, via Countryside and Glamour magazines of the 70s, all in addition to the numerous horror and thriller titles he is better known for.

Content includes Fiction (all imprints/editions inc. non UK) and Non-Fiction Categories: Horror, Thriller, Countryside and Children's Novels, Omnibus Collections, Chapbooks, Graphic Novels, Anthologies, Fanzines, Booklets, Magazines (70s adult Glamour, Country Sport, Game-keeping, Horror etc.), Periodicals and Newspapers.

The book also contains an original Guy N. Smith short story 'The Beast in the Cage' along with humorous insight into the levels of collecting Guy N. Smith's works in 'The Completist- A Cautionary Tale' by author Shane P.D Agnew.

The Sinister Horror Company is an independent UK publisher of genre fiction. Their mission a simple one – to write, publish and launch innovative and exciting genre fiction by themselves and others.

For further information on the Sinister Horror Company visit:

SinisterHorrorCompany.com
Facebook.com/sinisterhorrorcompany
Twitter @SinisterHC

SINISTERHORRORCOMPANY.COM

Milton Keynes UK
Ingram Content Group UK Ltd.
UKHW041055061124
450821UK00001B/1